THE YELLOW WOOD

MELANIE TEM

ChiZine Publications

FIRST EDITION

The Yellow Wood © 2015 by Melanie Tem
Cover artwork © 2015 by Erik Mohr
Interior design © 2015 by Jared Shapiro

Distributed in Canada by
HarperCollins Canada Ltd.
1995 Markham Road
Scarborough, ON M1B 5M8
Toll Free: 1-800-387-0117
e-mail: hcorder@harpercollins.com

Distributed in the U.S. by
Diamond Comic Distributors, Inc.
10150 York Road, Suite 300
Hunt Valley, MD 21030
Phone: (443) 318-8500
e-mail: books@diamondbookdistributors.com

Library and Archives Canada Cataloguing in Publication

Tem, Melanie, author
   The yellow wood / Melanie Tem.

Issued in print and electronic formats.
ISBN 978-1-77148-314-8 (pbk.).--ISBN 978-1-77148-315-5 (html)

   I. Title.

PS3570.E42Y44 2015   813.54   C2014-908374-2
                                            C2014-908375-0

bitlit

A free eBook edition is available
with the purchase of this print book.

CHIZINE PUBLICATIONS
Toronto, Canada
www.chizinepub.com
info@chizinepub.com

Edited by Andrew Wilmot
Proofread by Indrapramit Das

CLEARLY PRINT YOUR NAME ABOVE IN UPPER CASE

Instructions to claim your free eBook edition:
1. Download the BitLit app for Android or iOS
2. Write your name in **UPPER CASE** on the line
3. Use the BitLit app to submit a photo
4. Download your eBook to any device

Canada Council   Conseil des Arts
for the Arts   du Canada

We acknowledge the support of the Canada Council for the Arts which last year invested $20.1 million in writing and publishing throughout Canada.

ONTARIO ARTS COUNCIL
CONSEIL DES ARTS DE L'ONTARIO

an Ontario government agency
un organisme du gouvernement de l'Ontario

Published with the generous assistance of the Ontario Arts Council.

Printed in Canada

THE YELLOW WOOD

DEDICATION

For John Kubachko, my father, who knew what should be done in the world but couldn't do it himself, so gave it to me to do. Now, I'm grateful.

And, always, for Steve.

Prologue

Through the yellow wood where she has not been for thirty years, my daughter Alexandra is coming to me. From the yellow-grey stillness of my house, the house she grew up in and fled to live her own life—as if there ever has been such a thing—I hear her at the junction of the path she took to escape from me and the path I took a long time ago to protect myself. Neither of us made the wrong choice. Neither of our choices was entirely effective.

My heart beats in my throat, pulse a bit thready, rhythm slightly irregular. I cannot claim that the unreliability of the pumping of blood through my body is a result of either her absence or her imminence. I have been aware of it to one degree or another most of my life, and in old age it has become increasingly noticeable. But now, waiting for the daughter who could be thought of as both scion and prodigal, I indulge myself in a brief fancy that her hands are choking me, her wilfulness breaking my heart.

There was a time when she hated me. She thought she hid that from me. There was a time when she adored me, and we both revelled. Of all my children, this one has always stirred me most, with love, with rage and fear, with envy and disappointment. With hope.

I can't believe I'm doing this. At forty-fucking-nine years old, you'd think I'd be able to say no to my father. I don't have time for this. It's busy at work. Martin and the kids need me at home. I have better things to do than tramp through these woods. My knees and ankles hurt, and I'm short of breath; just being here makes me feel physically vulnerable, let alone all the emotional crap.

A branch slaps me across the neck and I break it off savagely. Cobwebs make my arms and lips sticky. Imagining the spiders, imagining the snakes and who knows what other creepy and, to one degree or another, dangerous animals I know must live in here, I'm afraid, and that pisses me off.

My sister and brothers and I spent many an hour playing in these woods, forts and stick horses and hide-and-seek and just wandering, just absorbing. I'd never let my kids be gone all day like that with no adult supervision, and I don't subscribe to the easy popular wisdom that the world is any more dangerous for kids now than it used to be. The dangers change with the times, that's all. Because nobody ever got seriously hurt in the woods, or in the creek where we swam every day in the summer with no thought of a lifeguard, those are happy and expansive childhood memories. They could just as easily be traumatic. We were lucky.

I'm not feeling especially lucky now. I'm also not feeling safe. Saying no to my father meant emancipation for me, meant I wouldn't be swallowed up by him after all. I would have a life of my own. My adolescence was verbally turbulent—we had some shouting matches, and more than a few mutual days-long pouts—but the stakes were too high for me to openly rebel. That's why I cut off all contact for most of my adult life.

All those years, I got his messages. Most of the time it was through my siblings, but sometimes guilt or an infuriating longing would just explode in my mind, for no good reason. I trained myself not to respond, which wasn't easy, which cost me, but was necessary for my own survival. So, here and now, will I survive this?

He's old, and not well. I'm told he needs me. And I need something from him, though I hate to admit it. Approval, still? Release? A message of some sort, a gift? It makes me crazy to need anything from him.

My sister and brothers keep telling me he won't

live much longer. Bullshit. Alexander Kove will live for fucking ever.

Rustling off to my right draws my attention to a zigzag uplifting of the leaf mulch, a tiny, purposeful, energetic motion of which only the effect is visible. A vole, no doubt. Nothing sinister. Nothing especially meaningful. It wouldn't take much to chase it down and squash it under the pitiable layers of decomposing organic matter it probably thinks are protecting it. I wouldn't ever have to acknowledge what it had been. I won't do that, of course, but it wouldn't take much. It wouldn't take much on the part of the victim, either. I can see myself in either role.

My father wants to see me. Like a good little girl, I'm obeying. Yes, Daddy. I'm coming, Daddy. Jump, you say? Sure, Daddy, how high? The son of a bitch is back inside my head, pulling at me, guiding me through this thin little forest that, in my memory at least, is always one shade or another of yellow. Now it's chartreuse, one of the colours of my dance costume when I was five. Cerise and chartreuse. I loved the words, proof that Daddy was already influencing me, or I was born with a nature like his. Chartreuse, a Day-Glo yellow-green, especially where the sun pops through.

I remember these woods in my skin. I remember this path, the path I took, in the blood coursing through my body, forking and forking into ever-smaller vessels that all serve the same aortal core, the same four chambers, the same pulse. I grew up with my father's voice in my head, my father's will on me in one form or another. Now, though I vowed I never would, I'm going back. Does that mean I'm stronger now, or succumbing? I've never loved or hated anybody the way I've loved and hated him.

What if I die here? It could happen. Death can come anywhere, at any time. What if I never see Martin and the kids again? What if I never leave these woods?

My three sons and my other daughter were easy children to raise. Even after Eva Marie left—not for parts unknown but for parts so well known as to constitute a cliché—to seek her destiny, which she did in fact find, since whatever we end up finding is by definition our destiny. They all live near enough to satisfy my fatherly and grandfatherly urges, and even if they were not family I might at times enjoy the company of most of them.

But this, this is the one.

My ankle turns and I catch myself on a branch that I might have known won't hold my weight, bends and breaks, takes me down. Disproportionately enraged, I curse the two pounds a year I've gained since I left here, the woods and the dampness and my father and my own weakness. He's doing it again.

I'm allowing him to do it again. He's taking over my life. He's insinuating himself into my thoughts. It's taken me all my life to get rid of him, and he's back before I'm even in his physical presence.

He's summoning me. And here I am, Daddy's little girl, wizard's familiar, a snake or an eagle or a panther on a leash.

Getting up isn't easy. By the time it's accomplished, I'm trembling and panting. Brushing off my jeans, I see tiny blue flowers in the crevices of roots and rocks, early summer flowers I wouldn't have noticed if I hadn't fallen, if I hadn't entered these woods in the first place. Yeah, well, fuck you.

Here's where the two paths split, or come together, depending on your point of view. The girl who stood at this intersection thirty years ago had already decided which way to go but needed to mark and savour and come to terms with the moment.

The woman I am now strides past without a pause. Okay, Daddy, Alexander fucking Kove, old man, wizard, you who gave me life and could take it away, you to whom I owe everything and nothing, you from whom long ago I could free myself only by breaking my own heart. I'm ready to take you on, once and for all. Here I come.

She is named after me—her mother's idea. From my other children I have heard she calls herself Sandi now, so few would guess her name is Alexandra. But it is.

I close my eyes and see her at the place where the paths diverge—or converge, depending on one's perspective. When she was learning the poem, she kept saying, "converge," "two roads converged in a yellow wood," because she recognized that word first. I would correct her. She would pout or argue or squirm to get up. I was patient, though sometimes I despaired. She finally got it right.

Her slight hesitation would not be perceptible to anyone but me, waiting here for her. She, of course, thinks she did not pause at all, just strides past the intersection toward this long, low yellow house where she grew up and that she left behind. And in fact I do admire her stride. She is strong, massive; she has gained a great deal of weight since I saw her last, and it will not be easy for me to adjust to having a large child. She has power she knows about and power she has not yet realized. She thinks she is ready to take me on, and in my estimation she is correct, which is why I dared call her to me now.

Feeling her approach, I force myself to stay in my chair in order to hoard my paltry energy until the last possible moment, so I can be on my feet, in the doorway, reasonably steady and clear when she gets here. I can *scarcely breathe. After thirty years, my daughter Alexandra is only minutes away.*

After thirty years, I'm only minutes away. The most incredible thing is how natural it feels—like dying, like being born—to be making my way along the rough and narrow path through the yellow woods as if I'd been doing it every day of my life, roots heaved underfoot and cobwebby branches in my face, up that last hill that always was a bitch. Coming up on the long, low yellow house, I find it smaller than I remember because, in numerous ways, I'm so much larger.

"He wants to see you, Sandi."

"What for?"

"He wants to see you. The rest of us are a dime a dozen, nothing special, but you . . . you're the one he wants to see."

"Well, you know what, Em? I don't want to see him. I've got a life. Husband, kids, job, you know?"

"Just get your ass back here, okay? So he'll shut up about it. He's not going to be able to live alone much longer, out there in the middle of nowhere. He's not going to be with us much longer."

"Yeah, right."

"Sandi, for Chrissake. You can spare a few days from your busy life to visit your father. He raised us, remember? You owe him."

But it wasn't Emily's words that got me here. It was his. His words in my head, where they've always been. His will. His design.

As she reaches the edge of the clearing, her heartbeat fills my ears. Branches snap. The odour of decomposing yellow-leaf mulch rises from under her feet. Voles burrow wildly underneath, making labyrinths whose purpose is utterly practical, no spiritual or magical or ecological significance at all as far as their creators are aware, only in the perception of the hyper-imaginative human observer. It distresses and gratifies me that she does not appear aware of the snake sweeping from side to side behind her, gliding alongside, sometimes blatantly leading the way.

The time has come. I struggle up out of my chair, gasping at the pain in my back and the vertigo that almost swirls me to the floor. For just an instant I do not know why I make my way across the room, only that I must. I open the door and carefully step out onto the damp yellow porch. And there she is.

There he is.

A tall, heavyset woman with a long stride and a solid presence in the wood, in the world. Though fair-skinned and light-eyed, she has come to look little like either her mother or me, and for just a moment I think: this is not my daughter. Either she is an impostor or I am. Can this be my daughter?

Grey in yellow light, small and frail and very old, but undeniably my father. My head spins from rage and pulsing love.

"Alexandra."

"Daddy."

Chapter 1

"Daddy's a bastard!"

Vaughn and Will hooted in surprise and admiration. Galen, the firstborn, couldn't completely suppress a grin, but mostly he was horrified. I don't know where Emily was. She doesn't figure in this flashback. I wasn't much more than seven or eight, so maybe she wasn't old enough yet to be out playing in the woods with us.

If I was seven, Eva Marie—our mother—had been gone about a year. One yellow Saturday morning she'd gathered us all together—no mean feat in itself—to tell us through sincere and utterly self-referential sobs that she wasn't a good enough mommy for such wonderful children so she was going away.

"Away?" I don't know who said that. It could have been any of us, except Galen, who wouldn't have asked. "Away where?"

"I don't know."

"Does Daddy know?"

"He doesn't know where I'm going, no."

"Does he know you're leaving us?"

"Yes."

"Did he say it was all right?"

She did leave us, and not for any reason we could figure out. As far as we've ever known, there was no other man, or woman. When we saw her over the years, there were never any other kids, putting the lie to our various theories as to which of us had been so rotten she couldn't stand it; I have always more or less secretly harboured the conviction that it was Vaughn. Or me.

She didn't die, though she may be dead by now, for all I know, may have died before she got away, her car rolling off a cliff (there were no cliffs anywhere nearby, but there should have been) and bursting into flames, her blood and burned flesh coursing through the woods—only one of my many fantasies. She didn't leave us because she died; she left of what could be called her own free will, though that's a slippery term. You'd think we'd all be neurotic about people leaving, and maybe my siblings are; my little sister had her share of anxiety for a while. What I'm neurotic about is death. The very illogic of it makes it harder to face, impossible to come to terms with. Maybe I thought I would die when she left.

Or maybe she's not responsible for this at all. Practically everybody's afraid of death. Maybe it's not her fault that there are times when I'm nearly incapacitated by it, nearly overcome. But pinning it on her has helped, and I see no reason to stop now.

She didn't seem crazy. She didn't seem like a bad person. She also didn't seem like a mother. She just left. Nobody else ever did, except me, and even doing that didn't tell me why she did. She had five kids. She just left us and never came back. That's pretty close to unforgivable. For the ones left, it's pretty close to dying.

It's also a clear event, one whose dimensions I've been able to get my mind around. I understand why I've always felt betrayed by her—because, in fact, she betrayed us. Why I've felt betrayed by our father—who was responsible, who raised us, who gave us more than any other parent I've ever heard of and yet harmed us in some mysterious and precious and vital way—has been harder to grasp and therefore harder to forgive.

"Daddy's a son of a bitch!" I was hollering, but the woods absorbed it all, allowing no echoes. If somebody had been far enough away to hear only the singsong without the words, I might have been calling, "Olly olly oxen free!"

Galen snorted. "You in trouble again?"

Our games were often elaborate, ongoing constructs, but that day I think we were just wandering in the woods, my big brothers and I. "No TV for a week. And I have to do extra chores."

"What'd you do this time?"

"Nothing."

"Little Miss Innocent."

"Didn't do her homework," Will or Vaughn was happy to supply.

The real reason I was in trouble was that I wouldn't accept what he'd decided it was time for him to give me. The gift. One of his cursed gifts.

I should never have told him about the girl in school everybody made fun of. Not that he wouldn't have known anyway; a lot of seven-year-olds believe their parents know everything, but Daddy really did. Still does. He might not have fixated on her though, if I hadn't brought her to his attention. The only way I was ever able to stop doing that, and then not completely, was, eleven years later, to go away and stay away.

"There's this girl in school. She talks funny."

"Penny Wyckoff."

"You know her?"

"You know her, Alexandra."

I must have mentioned her at some time or other. "She talks funny. She walks funny, too." I demonstrated Penny's lurching gait and mush-mouthed diction, making myself laugh.

"Alexandra, pay attention. You are not to mock her."

"Huh?"

"You may not make fun of her. Do you understand me?"

"Everybody makes fun of her. She doesn't mind."

"You will be the one who does not. You will be her friend."

"No, Daddy! Then they'll make fun of *me*."

"Alexandra. Tomorrow I want you to ask Penny to play with you. The Kove family *will* bring good into this world."

"No, I don't want to!"

"From now on, you will play with her at recess and eat lunch with her and sit with her on the bus."

Desperately: "I won't laugh at her anymore, okay? I just won't laugh at her!"

"Not adding to the bad things in the world is not enough for us. We will add to the good."

The "we" stirred me, even as I was infuriated by it. Daddy never reached out to anybody. Loving us was his limit, and even with us his love was fierce, inward, smouldering, about as far as you could get from expansive; I'd never seen him go out of his way to be actively kind. He was asking—ordering; compelling—me to do something he wouldn't do himself.

Well, I wouldn't do it, either. It wasn't fair. It was asking too much. I set my jaw. "Alexandra," he warned.

The next day I ignored Penny, didn't tease her or laugh when she tripped or mock the way she talked, didn't join in when other kids made fun of her. Didn't befriend her, either. Herpie, who'd been dispatched to see that I did as I was told, was with me all the way home, hissing and flicking her tongue and lidlessly glaring, her slithers and narrow loops like punctuation.

That's why I was in trouble.

I didn't tell my brothers any of that. Walking on the thin trunk of a fallen tree, holding out my arms and deliberately making it sway, I shrieked as if in play, "He says I was insolent!" Daddy had been careful to explain what the word meant; his not infrequent application of it caused me shame and pride, both secret from everybody but Daddy. And I liked being able to use the big word.

"What's that mean?" one of my brothers demanded.

"It means she got smart with Dad," another of them was glad to answer. "Talked back."

"It's good to be smart," I said, insolently. "Daddy wants us to be smart."

"Daddy wants *you* to be smart," Vaughn sneered, and blew on a blade of grass to make ferocious music.

Now I was chanting, "Daddy is a bastard, Daddy is a creep, Daddy is a shithead, Daddy is a bleep," skipping through the undergrowth as if I had a jump rope in my hands. It was, of course, to him that I owed the precocious facility with the language that allowed me to come up with this insolent rhyme.

"Alexandra, cut it out," Galen ordered.

"Daddy is a son of a bitch, Daddy is a jerk, Daddy is an asshole, Daddy is a—" I kept skipping and twirling my imaginary jump rope while I tried to think of a rhyme.

"Perv," Vaughn or Will suggested, giggling.

I fairly chortled, "Daddy is a perv." Inescapably my father's daughter, I was delighted by the wordplay more than by the meaning of the word, of which I had only a hazy grasp.

"Don't say that," Galen warned all of us. He broke off a branch as thick as a man's finger and as long as a man's arm and swung it menacingly at his side. Just under the flayed bark, the flesh of what I would much later learn was called the cambium layer was shockingly moist and green, and the bark peeled in a long, painful-looking streamer past the break, and all up and down the shaft were struggling little oval leaves that flashed yellow-green in the dappled sun.

The branch had been alive before he broke it and now, a split second later, was dead. It didn't yet look dead or, when I reached to touch it in Galen's hand and he let me take it from him, feel dead, but I understood that it was. Realizing what I'd just witnessed made me shudder. Galen would never have dared to do that if Daddy'd been with us. Daddy was always fiercely declaiming, "That branch, that spider, that ant, that weed has as much right to live as you do," though he couldn't restrain himself from killing spiders. I shivered again, wondering how much trouble Galen would be in when Daddy found out what he'd done.

"Everything living uses other living things. Even vegetarians consume the life force of other living things. There's no shame in that. But we don't take life lightly. We have to be aware."

I teach that to my own kids. Even the arachnophobes in our house suppress the urge to squash the spider on the wall so the arachnophiles can slide it into a jar and release it in the yard. The kitchen counter is often festooned with cans and banana peels until I can take care of them; nobody will join me in recycling or composting, but at least they aren't cavalier about throwing things away.

I got this reverence for life directly and consciously from my father. I have put my own spin on it and passed it on, set it loose in the world. Just as my father intended. But I've never really believed he himself revered life or anything else. He just thought I should.

Galen, Vaughn, Will, and Emily all understand something about the magic if not the sanctity of life. Galen resists the local cultural pressure to hunt and fish, and is active in political, social, and ecological causes in which it often appears I believe more than he does. Vaughn makes music, his flute or didgeridoo or bongo nearly a living creature in the near or distant wood. Emily started having babies at eighteen and did not stop until well into her forties; she does not find being a mother especially fulfilling, but she is good at it, her gift, her curse. In much the same spirit, Will gardens—out of duty far more than pleasure, but his tomatoes and roses are nonetheless sweet.

"Daddy is a robber, Daddy is a creep, Daddy is a—"

Of all of us, Alexandra is the one who goes out into the world. She always has; I sent her there, an emissary and standard-bearer, then lost my nerve for her and tried to pull her back where she would be safe, which naturally made her stay away with a vengeance. Sometimes I think I taught her wrong. Sometimes I allow myself pride.

"—wizard—"

It has been all I could do to love my father and mother, my wife, and my children. Never a friend, not my siblings or grandchildren, certainly not humanity as a whole. Considering where I started, this is no small feat. It is, however, insufficient. Therefore, I developed in Alexandra her natural ability to love expansively, to extend herself, to risk. That led her to marry a man I would never have chosen for her, an actual African from the continent of Africa, and to claim children who can only bring trouble.

"—Daddy is a thief."

I taught her to explore the wood, which, though I built my house and my family and my life here, frightens me enough that I have never ventured far into it myself. At three years old, her mother preoccupied, not to say over-whelmed, by the baby and I with what was taking shape in my wife's heart, Alexandra got lost in the woods for half a day. Her mother found her. I could not bring myself to go in there after her. Making a show of unity, as parents are supposed to do, we both shouted and both cried and both imposed a rule that she could no longer go outside the house without one of us. Alexandra looked at me, specifically me, as if I had betrayed her, and in important ways I had.

I was always wandering off into the woods and losing track of time and place. It drove my mother crazy, and now that I'm a mother I can understand why. If my kids did half the things I did, I'd have a fit. I never got lost, though, and was aware of only enough danger to make me feel brave.

In some way, I did it for Daddy. He'd be waiting anxiously on the front porch, and he'd scold or hug or shake me a little, but he'd also listen avidly to my tales of what I'd encountered or imagined in the woods. When I was very young, three or four, I'd bring things back to show Daddy—flowers I'd picked, bugs in a jar. He taught me not to impose my will, to let them be, to collect them only in words. "Centipede" is a nice word, and "buttercup." And "milk snake," which I realized only much later Daddy had sent slithering after me to guide me home.

If I told her how once upon a time I squandered magic, both others' and my own, she would know me better. I am not likely to tell her. It is tempting, in the way that jumping off a cliff is tempting even when one is not in the least suicidal, but I will resist. Even Alexandra, especially she, is not to know me that well.

Perhaps she already knows. Often power derives not from knowledge itself but from the means by which knowledge is transmitted. I have not told her, but perhaps she knows. Perhaps that is why she hates me, and has stayed away all these years. Perhaps that is why she has come back now. She is my daughter, my scion, my hope and gift to the world, whether she wants to be or not.

And having virtually no corporeal sense of her became unacceptable. Over the years she sent physical and, lately, electronic photographs, from which I gleaned she steadily put on weight, coloured and then stopped colouring her hair, married a black man—an African, but still a Negro—and adopted two older children of decidedly mixed race. Galen will make some comment about how old everybody's getting. Emily sniffs that it's sad how Sandi is letting herself go.

I still have gifts to give to Alexandra, whether she wants them or not. Explanations to make. Instructions to convey. To do all that, I must encounter her in the flesh. That is why I called for her. I do not know why she has come.

Vaughn and Will veered off the path to see what had grown or decayed under a particular log since the last time they'd looked. I kept chanting bad things about Daddy, but not out loud anymore; Daddy would never hit us, but Galen would. And, besides, Daddy could hear what I was saying inside my head. I made it as bad as I could, and he loved me anyway. The persistence of his love would, not a decade later, give me both the strength to leave him and the need to do so.

The other children have all resented me at one time or another. That goes with the parental territory. Will was a particularly rebellious teenager. I misjudged Vaughn's interest in music and pushed him too hard, so that for a while he had to give it up altogether in order to extract me from it and make it his own again. Galen and Emily routinely lose patience with me, but only Alexandra has ever hated me. Only Alexandra still does.

"Good morning, Daddy."

He's been standing in the doorway for the last few minutes, watching me write. Across the room and behind me, he nonetheless exudes the impression of reading every word I write, and as I've been stubbornly typing I've been distracted by the need to tell myself both that he can't possibly have access to my thoughts, and that since there's no way to conceal anything from him anyway I might as well finish the damn paragraph.

I keep trying to call him "Dad" or even "Father." For a while I was referring to him as Alexander. But his name to me is Daddy, and here, in his house, in the house I grew up in and escaped and despite all my best efforts have returned to, he won't answer to anything else.

He says good morning. I revise the last sentence, revise it back to what it was in the first place, save, exit, turn off the laptop. First oblique glimpse of my father as I swivel in the creaky chair to face him: a frail old man in a knee-length blue rayon robe, embarrassing because it shows his brittle shins, feet in ugly fake leather slippers awkwardly apart for balance, hands grasping the doorjamb on either side, shoulders hunched; eighty-one years of constriction etched in his face, the features of which I can't quite see for the backlight. Flooded with tenderness, I smile.

"Did you sleep well?" he asks me formally.

"Really well."

"Your old bed is still comfortable?"

"Very."

He nods. I nod. We share an awkward pause. "You are up early."

"So are you."

"Oh, I am up and down all night. And all day, for that matter." He hesitates, and I brace myself, knowing what he's going to ask before he asks it. "What are you writing?"

Because I've longed for him to be interested in my life, I've fiercely kept much of it from him. I'm relieved to be able to answer, "A major report for work. It's due by the end of the month."

Nodding and frowning, he turns away without asking what it's about, leaving me feeling suckered. "What would you like for breakfast?"

She is not about to ask me to read this report of hers, and I will not risk offering. Report writing is beneath her anyway. It is not what I gave her to do. She ought to be writing sonnets, dramatic tragedies, stories about the history and future of the universe. Disappointment causes me to turn away.

She says she would like coffee, and anything to eat except eggs. Toast, fruit, cereal, anything. French toast? I still make great French toast. (Remember?) This is not the best breakfast for someone overweight, but she says fine, and I shuffle off to the kitchen, pitiably pleased to be cooking for her again.

I hate French toast. I've always hated French toast, but it was his specialty so I could never bring myself to say so. Swamped and buoyed by the conviction that Daddy knew everything, I took this as evidence of his need to control, and of my collusion.

Whisking together eggs, slightly soured milk, cinnamon, and vanilla in a blue bowl, adding two pinches of the wild lavender that should not be a secret ingredient to her but probably is, I suddenly realize she is wondering if I might be poisoning her. The thought is fleeting and ludicrous, she gives it almost no credence, but she breaks my heart with it as only this child can do, and heartbreak makes me testy.

Poison? "What's that?"

"Lavender. You remember lavender."

"Are you sure it's safe to eat?"

"I have been using it for years. You know that."

Maybe that's why I couldn't stand his French toast, why French toast in general was ruined for me. My indignation is all out of proportion. "Maybe," I say wilfully, "that's why I've never liked French toast."

He stiffens. He turns from the stove. "You used to like it."

"No, I didn't." I'm in this now and can't back down.

"You ate it every Sunday morning for years. It was a tradition."

"I didn't want to hurt your feelings."

"So you deceived me." He didn't know. I always thought he knew and was deliberately forcing me to pretend to be someone I wasn't. He honestly didn't know, and now he feels tricked. The thought that I could trick my father is disorienting. I'm childishly ashamed, and childishly thrilled.

The stuff he's been whisking in the blue bowl goes into the sink. He scrapes out the pan, turns the garbage disposal on and off in a short, furious burst, runs soapy water for the abortively dirtied dishes to soak. "Help yourself to whatever you want for breakfast," he says with that terrible cold evenness. "You know where everything is," and he leaves the room.

I also didn't like learning Slovak just because we had relatives in the Old Country. Learning to write an approximation of the family name Kovalenko, before it became the decidedly non-Cyrillic Kove. I didn't like any of it, I complained and refused and held out against full restriction for weeks and weeks. But there was a secret satisfaction in it, too.

Daddy has left the room. He won't come back. I'll have to go after him, prostrate myself or at least apologize or at least make a conversational overture. Fuck that. I return to the bedroom and turn the laptop back on, intending to work on the conclusion of the report.

But he's done something to my head. "The man's a goddamn magician," I've told my husband more than once, raging, weeping, or chuckling wryly. "I swear he's got some kind of magic power."

"Of course he does." Martin doesn't believe in literal magic. He grew up in Cairo, went to boarding

school in Paris, admits to no tribal identity whatsoever. Because he knows something about powerful
fathers, having had one and being one himself, he
assumes I'm being metaphorical. That's what I'd have
said, too.

But here in my father's house, I am unable to write
what he scorns, what he would say is unworthy of
me. Of "us." Instead I take out the folders and the
disc where my novel and stories and poems that no
one has ever seen have been shaping and re-shaping
ever since I left this house. Under my father's spell, I
begin, haltingly, to write.

Chapter 2

Family. We are all family. The abused child, the black welfare mother, the panhandler with his sign plaintive ("haven't eaten in 5 days") or reasonable ("will work for food") or insolent ("you have $ and I don't how fair is that?") or outrageous ("will kill your mother-in-law for beer")—all are kin to each other and to my children and to me. Over the course of my life, with an effort no one else could appreciate, I have trained myself to believe that.

But I have not had the wherewithal to actually live that way. Until I built this house in this wood, I routinely encountered all sorts of beggars—knocking on our door during the Depression, ringing bells at Christmastime, soliciting over the telephone wire, coming too close to me on a city street—and I gave them money or I refused, either way because they made my skin crawl.

Personal connection is not my forte. I have never known how to talk to children, teenagers, women, Southerners, New Englanders, foreigners, the handicapped, the elderly. Other than the opportunistic alliances of childhood, I do not know that I have ever actually had a friend. Blacks, Mexicans, Orientals, Jews are perfectly fine people, but they are not my people.

This is not simple hypocrisy. My personal weakness, moral and otherwise, in no way diminishes what I know to be right and necessary in this world. I am ashamed that I cannot practice what I preach. I am proud to have carried the torch as far as I was able and then passed it on.

Loving the few individuals I have loved has been all I could do. I do not even try to keep straight everyone who can legitimately claim to be part of my family, many of them gathered here and now to celebrate Alexandra's homecoming. Grandchildren marry and divorce before I can learn their spouses' names. Great-grandchildren are several degrees too far removed to hold my attention. I keep wanting to call Galen's new wife Virginia or Valerie, but I believe it is Vivian; he is nearly sixty and she not much younger, so the concept of them being first-time newlyweds, though accurate, is counterintuitive.

Alexandra is showing photographs of her husband and children. I do not look at them. He is black. The children they adopted are not really my grandchildren. I am not obligated to remember their names. Loving them would be asking too much. She has always asked too much of me.

The unwelcome thought strikes me that Eva Marie would have known who all these people are and how they relate to each other. All the evidence is to the contrary, of course; she has not been part of this family for a long time. Even when there were only seven of us, it was too much for her. But the thought persists, then is replaced by a truer one: Alexandra is the one who knows, because I have asked it of her.

"You have a beautiful family," Emily tells me warmly.

"I do, don't I? Thanks." I am beaming.

Will wants to know, or at least he asks, "How old are your kids?"

"Thirteen and almost twenty."

"The girl's only thirteen? She looks older."

"My daughter, your niece, Tara, turned thirteen in January." It's obvious he doesn't get my point, but Emily does.

"I always have trouble telling the ages of—" Emily glares at him, but he's already stopped himself.

"That's okay," I say jovially. "Martin says he has trouble telling white people apart, too. We all kind of look alike."

There's uncomfortable chuckling. Then Will asks, "How old were they when you got them?"

"My son was twelve and my daughter was seven when they came to us."

"Have you had trouble with them?"

We have, but it seems a betrayal to say so to him. I shrug. "It's an adventure."

Emily sighs dreamily. "It's wonderful what you and Martin have done. Taking in kids who need homes.

It makes me proud to be your sister."

Both her admiration and my pride in it make me snippy. "We get as much as we give."

"You're heroes."

"We're parents, Emily. These are our children."

"Why didn't you have your own?" That's Vaughn, who has no kids.

Emily jumps in. "Vaughn, for God's sake, maybe they can't—"

"As far as we know we can. We chose to adopt. And Tara and Ramon *are* our own."

"You know what I mean."

"Yes," I tell them all, especially Daddy who hasn't said a word, "I know exactly what you mean."

Galen is characteristically the first to lose patience. "Don't be so touchy, Alexandra. You always were so damn touchy."

This is my fault. The trouble she has deliberately brought into her life, the risk she is taking, are direct results of how I brought her up. Intending to give her a gift, I have cursed her. Meaning to teach my child to be more than I could be, imagining her as my masterpiece and gift to the world, I have put her in danger. I can scarcely look at her.

"It's good to have you home," Emily says quietly to me. "I've really missed you."

This isn't home. Home is with my husband and my

children, in a city far away. "I've missed you, too, Em," and as I say it missing her comes flooding over me so I'm not really lying.

"Nobody calls me Em but you."

"Oh, sorry."

"No." Shyly, she touches my shoulder. "No, I mean, it's your special big-sister nickname for me. It's nice to hear it again."

"Are you happy, Em? I mean, overall, with your life?"

Her hand goes to her distended belly. She looks around at the assembled crowd, much of which she's directly responsible for. "I don't know about happy. That's a little strong. I'm content. That's enough for me. Most of the time." She glances at me, glances away. "Sometimes I wonder what it would have been like to do something else." I see how tired she is. "Then I feel guilty."

"Yeah. Me, too."

"You, too? Really? You wonder what your life would have been like if you'd taken a different path?" This time her glance is coy. "Stayed here, for instance?"

"That was one of Daddy's favourite poems." This is a diversionary tactic. It also feels like a sudden revelation, as if I hadn't remembered about the poem.

" 'The Road Not Taken.' Robert Frost." I'm surprised and not entirely pleased that she knows what I'm talking about. Despite having all these kids and living out here in the boonies, my little sister is not the rube I'd like to make her out to be.

We recite a few lines together and chuckle. Cautiously, I ask her, "Did you have to memorize it, too?"

"Oh, no, not me. You were his poetry buddy. I just learned it from listening to you."

She's challenging me, and we both hear the defensive edge in my voice when I counter, "I can't imagine why he liked that particular poem so much. He's led a pretty constricted life, if you ask me. He certainly didn't take the road less travelled by, that I know of."

"But you did. So he didn't have to." That snotty tone takes me back twenty-five years.

A chill runs through me. I rub my arms. "Well, anyway, all paths lead through the same woods. Or some such bullshit."

"What in the world does *that* mean?"

"Beats me. Sounds profound, though, don't you think?"

For a long beat she stares at me. Then we burst into riotous laughter that quickly has less to do with the amusement of the moment than with shared history and sweet old habit and older love. She puts her arm around me. I lean my head on her shoulder.

Herpie coils in the weeds at the edge of the yard. To say she is glaring would be to anthropomorphize, but I do feel her concentrated, lidless gaze. I have not consciously summoned her, and I have in mind no particular task for her at the moment, but I am neither surprised nor displeased to find her here. She is, in a word, familiar.

Eva Marie had an absurd terror of snakes. Of caterpillars, and night crawlers, too, and I trust that Vaughn's green horned tomato worms or an eel if she had ever seen one would have elicited the same slapstick response. She shrieked. She hooted. She flapped her elbows and hands. She hopped on one foot and then the other. She climbed atop rocks and stumps, the hood of the car, the swaying porch rail. Once, when the boys not entirely by accident spilled their bucket of fishing worms in the kitchen, she climbed in her nightgown onto the counter. It was hard not to laugh. Even now, those memories make my lips twitch.

Although she did not say so, it seems plausible that Eva Marie left because of Herpie. She would not share her husband with anything cold-blooded and legless.

"Are you happy, Em?" I press.

"I think this is the life I was meant to live."

"Meant? By whom?"

"Oh, you know. God. The universe. Fate."

"Daddy?" Realizing I've been holding my breath, I'm careful to exhale gradually.

"I don't think Daddy much cared what any of us did with our lives except you."

"Em."

"Well, it's true."

One of her daughters, Eileen or Eve, steps up onto the deck carrying glasses of iced lemonade. A pretty, disdainful girl, she just stands there. "Thanks, hon." Unable to reach the tray, Emily flails with one hand in a gesture that's supposed to be comic but clearly disgusts her daughter. "Come closer, come closer. I can't reach over your little sister or brother here."

A furious blush colours my niece's neck and face. She hands her mother one glass and me the other, then stalks off, wiping her hands on her white shorts. Emily sighs and shakes her head. "The mere fact of this baby's existence embarrasses her to death. The mere fact of *my* existence embarrasses her to death."

"It's the age. She'll get over it."

"I suppose."

"Too bad we didn't have a mother to embarrass us when we were that age."

"You've never heard from her, have you?"

"No. Em. I'd have told you." She doesn't answer. I can't let this go. "Emily, do you hear me? I wouldn't have kept something like that a secret from you and the boys."

"Okay." But she is not entirely convinced.

"Why do you suppose she left?" I don't think we've ever directly asked each other this question. Even now,

41

it's less a real query than a conversational gambit, an effort to claim and hold my sister's attention.

She's thought about this. She answers readily, looking not at me but at the family thronging our father's yard, which is really no more than a clearing in the woods. "I think the very fact of our existence embarrassed her to death."

It strikes me that this might be a clue of some sort. "To death?"

"Give me a break, Sandi, it's just a figure of speech."

"Well," I say, intending to chuckle wryly but coughing instead to clear the telltale constriction in my throat, "I guess the good news and the bad news is that there wasn't a lot we could do about the fact of our existence."

"I thought about it. Don't tell me you didn't, too." Her tone is conspiratorial, almost breezy, as if the memory we're sharing here is innocent and sweet.

"Thought about what?" I want her to say it. We hold each other's gaze for a long moment. Finally, characteristically, I'm the one who names it. "Suicide?"

Something across the clearing gives her an excuse to look away, and she leans forward, calls to one of the kids to stop that.

"Emily? Are you saying you thought about suicide?"

"Sure. Didn't you?"

"No!"

Not having expected the ambush, I don't get out of

the way fast enough. "You wouldn't. You're Daddy's girl."

Our mother used to say that all the time. After she left the others took it up, Emily especially. I hate it when I cry out of anger. Resisting the urge to punch her even if she is a pregnant woman, or to stomp into our father's house and shut myself in, I settle for snarling "Fuck you!" in the vicious undertone only siblings can achieve with each other.

"Watch your mouth," she reminds me with a smug equanimity that further infuriates me. Just like when we were kids and she, the little sister, had a better handle on things than I did. I flip her off in the private space between our two chairs, where nobody else can see. Unfortunately, she doesn't see, either.

Daddy's in the chaise lounge at the other end of the deck. His eyes are closed. I flip him off, too.

Adrift. The fatigue has unmoored me from time and place and purpose. Everything I have discovered and invented for keeping the world in order has melted, the spells and incantations and images and poetry, and I am adrift.

Someone says, "Daddy?"

Right at that moment, I don't know how to answer to that name.

"Daddy? Are you all right?"

I do not recognize the voice. I do not recognize this sun-hatted, double-chinned, broad-shouldered woman.

43

For just a second I do not recognize the name she calls me. I am so tired. "I have something to show you," *says my daughter Alexandra, shy and excited as a child, glancing up and then down from under her broad-brimmed hat. Out of her pocket she pulls something, a letter, an airmail letter, and holds it out for me to take. I do not accept it.* "It's a surprise," *she tells me, the very idea of which exhausts me even more. I do not ask what it is, but she presumes to inform me anyway.* "It's a letter from your relatives in the Old Country. Our family."

"Oh!" *Indeed, I am surprised, mostly pleasantly although there is also a frisson of dread. She wants me to take the letter from her hand, but that is asking too much.* "How did they find you?"

"I found them. For the past few years I've been doing a little detective work, and I finally found them. I wrote to them months ago and didn't hear back, and I thought it was the wrong family, or they weren't there anymore, or they weren't interested in corresponding with their American relatives." *She is talking too much. There are too many words. I am assaulted by her eager words.* "But just a few days before I left to come here, this letter came." *She flaps it at me, then gives up and pulls the flimsy letter out of the flimsy envelope.* "Here, I'll read it to you."

I do not have enough energy to hear this letter, or any other missive from any other source. But I also do not have the energy to escape. She settles herself and reads.

She is a good reader if I do say so myself, although she still tends to rush. "Slow down," I interrupt to instruct her. She does not like it, but she does as I say, and for a while I luxuriate in the rhythm and timbre of her voice, bequests from me and, in the circular way of so many things, hers back to me. She could be reading Keats or Aldous Huxley or the morning paper.

He's not paying attention. He's not interested. I put a lot of time and effort into finding these long-lost relatives for him, because he used to say he'd like to travel to the Old Country someday and meet his father's family. I even thought maybe we could go together. This was meant as a gift. He doesn't get it. He doesn't accept it. I read the letter anyway, goddammit, but I might as well have saved my breath. Daddy is a son of a bitch.

Too much. I do not know these people. Alexandra can do this. I cannot. It is not required of me. Alexandra can reach out into the world. I am gratified to see that she can, but I do not have to like it, and I certainly do not have to do it with her.

Emily's shadow falls across us. The word "akimbo" has always amused me, and her arms are akimbo now, heels of her hands pressed against her lower back. "What's that?"

"It's a letter from our relatives in Slovakia."

"Really? Wow! Daddy, you've always said—" Her face goes ashen and she catches her breath.

"Em? Emily? You okay?"

She nods, but it's a moment before she can speak. "I've been having sharp pains the last couple days. Two or three in a row and then they stop."

"Contractions?" Her due date is September 15, three more months.

A bevy of children, most of them hers, bursts out of the house. From his station at the barbecue grill, Earl yells at them to settle down. They don't. When I look back at my sister, colour has returned to her face and she's on her way to tend to the problem.

"Would you like something to drink, Daddy?" He moistens his lips but doesn't answer. He is goddamn going to answer me. "Daddy. Do you want something to drink? Ice tea? Lemonade?"

"I would like a beer, please."

"A beer?"

He opens his eyes and fixes me with a pale grey stare. "Would you like to see identification, Alexandra?"

Before I check the refrigerator for beer, I tear the letter into four pieces, all of which could still be read if anyone ever cared to try, and toss them into the trash can under the sink.

Chapter 3

She does not write. How can this be? She writes only reports and memos for the companies she works for, the occasional newsletter article. This is not art. She creates no beauty, expresses no horror, nothing new or important. Nothing that will mark her passage through this world, or mine.

Who does she think she is? This is not what I raised her to be. This is not why I sacrificed and suffered. I could have taken the easier and safer route and just not bothered to train a sinecure and standard-bearer for everything I have always prized but been too weak to act upon. Connections to other people. Expansive love. Tolerance. Writing. I could have just given up and let it all abort.

Instead, with enormous cost to myself, I gave it to Alexandra, the child among all my children who had more than ordinary potential. And she has squandered it. She has betrayed my trust.

Reading aloud to my father is almost more than I can bear. Almost more than I'm willing to bear, because it makes me so vulnerable to something he set in motion before I can remember, long before I had any choice in the matter. Something that started bright and dark and tangled between us and then spread out and came loose and is now folding back over.

Folding back over me, at least, suffocating me, pinning me down. The effect on him is no clearer to me than it's ever been. He's impassive in his chair, hands on scrawny thighs. Whenever I'm brave enough to glance at his face, his only expression is that impacted expressionlessness I never have been able to decipher. Yellow-grey bands of sunlight through the dusty slats of a window shade move across his cheek, forehead, bald head. Three weeks, actually twenty-two days, I've been back here—three times as long as I told Martin I could tolerate, a million times longer than I'd ever have expected—and nothing, nothing has made itself clear.

I've always loved reading aloud and being read to. I adore books on tape and author readings, and much prefer staged readings to fully mounted plays. When public radio airs storytelling or cowboy poetry or a segment from somebody's new novel, I pause in whatever I'm doing to revel in it. Everything I write I read aloud, even the most pedestrian of inter-office memos, and often I have my assistant read the more substantial things to me so I can judge how my words play in another voice.

Reading to each other—poetry, prose poetry, essays; any form short enough to accommodate interruptions of other, related sorts of passion—was a mainstay of my brief, sweet courtship these many years ago with the man who became my husband. Martin was and is a wonderful reader in several languages, and an equally accomplished listener. Reading still soothes when one of us is sick or sad or frantic about the kids or too tired to sleep, still is all of a piece with the numerous other passions of our marriage.

Reading aloud to Ramon and Tara, well past the age when most parents are relieved and sad that most kids have outgrown it, helped us make up for time lost among us. Long legs dangling, they'd sit on our laps for bedtime stories, and to this day their father's voice reading can calm them like nothing else. Maybe they'll read to their children, my father's legacy passed along to generations he refuses to claim.

I had children of my own before I could acknowledge that my love of reading aloud and being read to came from my father. Of all the things he imposed on me, this one is most my own, so fundamental a part of me that I might have been born with it. He must have read to me when I was an infant, maybe when I was still in the womb—an image that for a long time has given me the creeps. The discovery that I'm grateful to him, here in his dingy and shimmering yellow living room, stops me short. He waits for me to go on. Or maybe he's asleep.

I am remembering. Harbouring no illusion that this scene is occurring here and now, I nonetheless give it my full attention, so that to an outside observer I doubtless appear out of touch with reality.

"What's this?" This was my cousin's son, therefore my cousin in some degree, a boy about two years younger than I named Roger. We shared a room. I shared his room. I was an interloper in his room. My cousins had agreed to keep me for a few weeks until my parents recovered from the influenza. My parents did not recover. My cousins had not committed to rearing another child, and they did not. They allowed me to live among them. They fed and clothed me, and they were not unkind. But it would have been too much to expect them to give me a home.

Just after I had met Eva Marie, Roger showed up at the door of my rented room on Hudson Street. He was a salesman, of kitchenware if I remember correctly. He was just passing through. We spent a mildly pleasant hour. The fact that we had grown up together, in the same room in the same house if not really in the same family, supplied us with no more than an hour's worth of things to talk about. I have not thought about him since. Now I am remembering him when he was ten years old.

"Something I wrote," I answered him, neither proud nor embarrassed, merely matter-of-fact. "Poems."

"Wrote?" Roger was never the most sophisticated youngster. "Poems?" He shuffled the papers, squinted. "You mean you made it up?"

I was studying. Algebra or chemistry, something with formulae, and did not want to take the time to complain about him rifling through the drawer that had been designated for my use, especially since I had objected before and he could not seem to stop himself. He began to read aloud, my words in his flat voice. I kept my pencil working and my head bent over the symbols on the paper, but I listened intently to Roger's halting, monotonic rendering of words that had come from the marrow of my bones. It was a poem about winter.

It was terrible. Insipid and clumsy, not a flash of talent or originality in it. By the time he reached the last overwrought phrase, I was in despair. I finished the problem I was working on, laid my pencil on the desk, did not look up.

Roger said, "Wow, Alex. You're a genius." And I knew then he could not be trusted.

The mere act of reading aloud to my father moves me so that I can sometimes barely get the words out, and I've avoided content that would carry its own filial associations. No Frost or Dickens or Keats; no poetry of any kind. Not the Gettysburg Address, either; I can still recite every word ("Four score and seven years ago . . ."), and once it gets started it has the obsessive quality of a pop song stuck in my mind (". . . our fathers brought forth on this continent a new nation,") or a spell he's laid on me ("conceived in liberty, and dedicated to the proposition . . ."). Maybe someday I'll recite it for him (". . . that all men are created equal."). He might like that. I'd never know whether he did, but he might.

Not yet. We're not there yet. It cost me more than enough just to propose, "Shall I read to you, Daddy?"

His pale grey gaze swung toward and past me, a balloon limp on a string. Was it "read" he didn't understand, or "I" and "you" in the same phrase? Or had I said something wrong, something he couldn't or wouldn't tell me but would hold against me for the rest of our lives?

Stubbornly, I insisted, "Daddy. Would you like me to read to you—"

"Yes." He answered without even a normal conversational beat.

I ought to be used to this from him. Not being listened to, not being able even to influence the course of any interaction, was a basic theme of my childhood. The ancient rage feels very present, and necessary. For a man as conversant with the various realities in the world as my father purports to be, he's remarkably disinterested in anything anybody else has to say, especially his family, especially me, expecting instead that he'll impart and I'll kowtow to his wisdom and instruction. What an asshole. What a charlatan.

"Yes," he repeated, even in his confusion seizing the upper hand. Primal rage, what a therapist once termed "fear of engulfment," propelled me to my feet, typescript in hand, intending to stalk out of the room and just leave him there. Then the word skipped away from him like a wilful child, and his head kept up a pale nodding and "yes" got free of any semantic mooring and just kept going "yes yes yes yes yes."

I sat back down and took a breath. Was I capitulating or for once imposing my will? "This is something I'm working on. I thought you might find it interesting."

Up to then I'd been willing to risk nothing more personal than the newspaper, and only parts of that. This was the next increment. Either he didn't know what was at stake or he didn't care. He smiled with vague, insulting beneficence. I'd thought myself long past caring what he knows or what he cares about. Apparently not. Grimly, I began.

"Alexandra, pay attention. Slow down. Alexandra. Slow down. Pay attention to each sound in each word. Articulate. Don't miss anything."

I have been duped. I thought she was going to read to me something that mattered, something to show what she has done with this gift. The episode with my cousin Roger demonstrated once and for all that I had neither the talent nor the discipline to be a writer. So I gave it to her. And she has wasted it on personnel memos and newsletter articles about some kind of new floor covering her company is hawking.

My own gift—from whom or what I could not say—is awareness of possibilities and obligations. Alexandra has that, too. My curse is being afraid of almost all of it. Alexandra was not to be afraid.

"Lower your voice. It is too much in your head. Lower. Deeper. Slower. Now, read that paragraph to me again. Again."

What I read to him is a long memo to H.R. analyzing options for a new benefit package. When I pause to make a note in the margin, he says, "There's a poem I've always liked. 'Come live with me and be my Love.' Do you know it?"

"Yes." He isn't *listening*. Imagine that.

"How does it go?"

I won't play. "I haven't memorized it."

" 'Come live with me and be my love—' "

"Did you recite that to Ma?" The question is decidedly truculent, not to mention impertinent. I don't take it back, and he doesn't answer it. I hear music. "What's that?"

Vaughn's drum and then his flute sound from deep in the woods. Alexandra frowns. "What's that?"

"That is Vaughn's music."

"Vaughn is more than a little eccentric, isn't he? Was he always like that?"

Daddy looks at me as if I'm speaking Martian, the way my kids do when I intrude on their important thoughts with questions about stupid things, like where they're going and when they'll be home. Ramon is particularly good at that blank look, and it never fails to piss me off.

What is Vaughn? Is that a name of a person or of an object that has slipped my mind? Who is this person asking me this incomprehensible question? Why is she peering at me as if I am an alien? Perhaps I am an alien. Where am I?

Alexandra, my daughter, is asking me about her brother my son Vaughn's music. That makes perfect sense. "He showed an appreciation of music quite early on."

"You used to listen to classical music all the time. Ma made fun of it."

We will not speak of her mother. "Vaughn listens to those old records. He refurbished the eight-track tape player so he could listen to my tapes."

"So he got his love of music from you?"

"Yes."

"How?"

I allow myself not to understand what she means. It does not take much.

"Did you give it to him? Did you force it on him? Inject it, or mix it into his food or something?"

Her snort is both unattractive and disrespectful. I allow a silence after it, so as to highlight her misstep. Then I tell her, "I have always admired people who create music. You may recall that you used to sing."

"Not very well. And I hated the lessons. Does Vaughn enjoy making music?"

"Enjoyment is irrelevant. He creates music because he must. Music is a valuable thing in the world, and I am not able to create it, so he must." This is entirely too revealing. I will myself to retreat into confusion again, but do not.

Something like horror niggles at the back of my mind. I don't understand what's going on here, and before I can think of what more to say to him about it, he's asleep. I sit there with him for a while, for no good reason, and then I leave the room. I leave the house, going nowhere in particular, just getting away from my father without, of course, ever really getting away.

She is gone. I do not know how long she has been gone, but the sensation is of years. I do not know, have no way of gauging how long she will be gone. I count thirty seconds

56

as if for the thunderclap, and then pry myself out of the chair and set myself in motion to the room that was once hers—temporarily, as it turned out—and is now temporarily hers again. At the T of the hallway I first turn the wrong way, going toward my room instead of hers, but righting myself requires only a small adjustment.

The door opens readily, of course; it has never had a lock, though somehow I expected more resistance. I step inside, close the door behind me, then open it again so as to hear her re-enter the house. My own canniness excites me, and I disapprove of the excitement.

Her presence is everywhere in here. The bed is unmade. On the dresser are toiletry items, a clock radio, two bottles of what I first think in some alarm are medications but on closer inspection turn out to be vitamins, and a framed 5" x 7" colour photograph of Alexandra, her husband, and the two children they adopted, all four of them strangers to me in this flat form.

She has set up her computer on the desk, which strikes me as rather more presumptuous than an open notebook would have been. The black briefcase beside it contains papers having to do with her work, utterly prosaic and predictable. Various cords and plugs and arcane devices, presumably computer-related, jumble together on the desk and on the floor.

When I open the bottom drawer, it nearly falls out and catching it wrenches my back. In it are packets of letters, bound with rubber bands and labelled. I recognize

*names of old friends I have not thought of in decades,
couples with whom Eva Marie and I socialized, a former
neighbour with whom I walked in the woods and talked
politics. Other names mean nothing to me. The name
on the thinnest packet is Bill Petrovsky, and after a long
moment it comes to me that he was a childhood playmate.*

*When Alexandra was in grade school, her best friend
was a little crippled girl from town named Penny. I believe
the name was Penny. The sight of the child sickened me.
I insisted Alexandra invite Penny over to spend the
night, and invite her again. I indoctrinated her in the
importance of friendship—something in which I, a fun-
damentally lonely man, believe in with grim fervour. I
instilled in her a need to reach out to the underdog in
fiercely personal ways.*

*The girls were close as long as Alexandra lived here.
Penny, who stayed in town, mentions to my other children
that she and Alexandra still carry on a lively epistolary
relationship via letter and email. I take credit for that.*

*But now I stare in something like horror at all these
correspondences with people she would consider friends
of mine, who are, of course, not my friends because I have
never had the capacity for friendship. Worse even than
that missive from the Old Country, they appal me, and
I know I taught her wrong.*

The yellow woods don't hold a goddamn thing for
me. I can't imagine why I ever thought it would. It's

full of him. It shuts me out while at the same time demanding that I go in. Every path either dead-ends or takes me back toward the house. Fuck this. Vowing to avoid anything that even remotely resembles a path, I strike out into brush and trees and undergrowth, across uneven ground, between and over rocks both deeply embedded and loose underfoot, through water running and stagnant that immediately seeps into my shoes. Simultaneously and ludicrously, I feel like a hopelessly defiant child and an intrepid explorer. To the narrow, herding slither ahead and beside and behind me and sometimes even over my head, I announce more than once, "Fuck you, Herpie," inordinately gratified by the ridiculous name.

The second drawer sticks. I tug it open. Inside is a box. I remove it, knowing full well that it will contain only more evidence of how she is wasting her life. The lid loosens easily. Yellow light through the window at my back illuminates page after page of typescript. Alexandra has written a novel.

This is what I have been waiting for all her life. Now, faced with it, holding it in my hands, I am filled with equal parts dread and exhilaration, fury and shame and pride.

I cannot read it now, although I will. I will re-enter this room repeatedly when she is gone (there is nothing shady about that; this is my house), carefully remove the manuscript box from the desk drawer where she has stored it as if preparing to show me or for me to find (this part—going through her personal effects—is inarguably dishonest, disrespectful, reprehensible), and read it page by page, chapter after chapter, by turns bearing in mind and putting out of my mind the fact that the author is my daughter Alexandra, who I thought had rejected this gift. "People can give you shit," she used to say impudently, staring straight at me or ostentatiously looking away, "but you don't have to take it," as though my legacy were waste.

I will read it. But now, at this first encounter, I regard the manuscript as artifact, and take inventory of its physical characteristics. Its heft and thickness; the number in the upper right-hand corner of the last page is 412. Its neatness. Its finished quality; no indication of being a work in progress. Its title, *Fatherland*, which gives me chills, and the author's name, Alexandra Kove—not her married name or nickname but the name her mother and I gave her.

Willing and able to take only so much of this at one time, I replace the lid on the manuscript box. I am an old man, and not well; strong emotion is more dangerous to me now than ever. I will require some time and effort to come to terms with the mere knowledge that this manuscript exists and has been brought into my house. I put it back. In the small drawer above it are tools of a trade that was never mine but that I claim in some sort of stubborn way that could be called metaphorical but is

*probably just irrational: computer discs, note cards, a
new box of black razor-point pens. My daughter is more
a writer than I have ever been.*

*All this time, she has taken what I have given her and
made it her own. This is what I intended. This is what I
hoped for and thought would never happen.*

How dare she?

By now I'd have expected to come across somebody's house—if not Daddy's then one of my siblings',
at least Vaughn's cabin. These woods aren't all that big.
Aware of the first buzz of nervousness in my chest,
I realize I could get lost here of all places. Where's
Vaughn's fucking music when I need it? Where's
the snake?

I stumble and bang my knee against a sharp stump.
Nothing on any side of any tree looks like moss, but
locating north wouldn't do me any good anyway,
since I don't know what's north of where I am. Weak
sunlight through the tree canopy doesn't seem to
me to have changed at all since I've been out here,
which makes sense when I check my watch and see
that I've been gone from my father's house less than
forty-five minutes.

Panting from this minimal physical exertion, and
from disproportionate fear, I sit down on a swaying
log to catch my breath and find myself at eye-level
with a rocky overhang. Under it is a cave. Inside

the cave are objects, most as grey as the rock itself but some of them bright white in the slanted and filtered sunlight.

Hearing in my mind my husband's frequent remonstrance, "Sandi, you're going to get yourself hurt someday, the chances you take," and ignoring it this time as he believes I always do, I slide off the log, snagging my pants. On my hands and knees, I inch forward. To the faint welcoming or warning hiss, I actually say aloud, "Oh, Herpie, go fuck yourself," and chuckle at the image, a nasty variation on the snake with its tail in its mouth.

The space under the rock is deeper than I'd have thought possible. Inside the lip of the overhang it widens into a tiny, close room in which I can sit cross-legged and not be grazing wall or ceiling. It's no cooler in here than outside, humidity diffusing the heat everywhere. The entrance, which is also the only exit, is a horizontal gash halfway around the very close horizon. It's like being inside a mouth. "Oh, please," I deride myself, and my flat voice goes nowhere.

On the dirt floor of the cave is a notebook. Filled with my father's handwriting, harder to read than ever. Just looking at it makes me shiver as I always did, makes me imagine secrets and spells. These appear to be something like lab notes, records of the same experiment conducted repeatedly, and from the dates on some of the entries, over a period of years. Some of the ingredients are vaguely familiar, at least by name—mothballs, fleabane, brown recluse venom, digitalis. Others seem to be in another language. "Slow poison," says one notation, letters so minimally formed it's virtually a straight line. Another: "Should take two or three weeks." And, "Will resemble death from natural causes, old age, etc."

What is this? I flip through the pages again. On the inside front cover, where I hadn't noticed it before, I now see a tiny printed title: SUICIDE PLAN.

As quickly and carefully as I can, knowing I'm making mistakes, I replace everything I've disturbed except the yellow pad. This, my father's suicide plan, I take with me as I scramble out of his hideout. Curses, Daddy. You've been foiled again.

Chapter 4

"Maybe he molested you when you were too young to remember it but it's all in there and it's ruined your life and that's why you were always his favourite and that's why you stayed away for so long." My sister's blue-grey eyes are gleaming, and when she leans cumbersomely toward me I can smell raspberry tea and eagerness on her breath.

"You saw that on Oprah, right?"

"*And* Sally Jessy *and* Jerry Springer."

"Must be true then."

"It doesn't make it not true. Clichés have their roots in truth."

Who knew my sister would turn out to be this complicated, contradictory, exasperating, fascinating woman? Neither her vapidity nor her insightfulness ever ceases to amaze me. Over the years she's been my main source of information about the family: Will's gardening misadventures and Galen's latest rally at the courthouse and Vaughn's increasing weirdness and her endless attempts to find the right colour bedspread and our father's declining health and the weather no more or less predictable than when we were kids—all receiving the same emphasis. I used to tune out her chatter, but I've come to realize I miss important things that way, details and patterns nobody but Emily has noticed, clichés that have their roots in truth.

She's never mentioned that our father has a detailed plan for killing himself, and to all appearances, the means to do it. It doesn't seem the sort of thing Emily, of all people, would keep quiet about. Most likely she doesn't know. I ought to tell her, of course.

But maybe I'm wrong. Maybe I'm jumping to conclusions. That would be embarrassing. Maybe it's not my place to tell any of these people—my "family"— anything about each other, since I don't have a context and the history I share with them is ancient. In most ways I'm not one of them. Or, maybe, I just want to have a secret with Daddy. I wouldn't like to think that, but it could be true.

For whatever reason, I have said nothing about what I found a week ago today in Daddy's hideout, and I say nothing about it now, choosing to pursue a safer subject. "I don't think he ever molested me, Em. I have thought about it, but I don't have any symptoms of an incest survivor." I stop short of saying that I do think there's some other deep dark family secret.

Today we're on Emily's patio. The family has gathered for yet another barbecue. These people love barbecues. Personally, I've never understood the appeal. Next week there'll be a barbecue in honour of the Fourth of July, and I'll miss my kids and fireworks over City Park lakes at home. The woods here have been chopped back to clear a neat rectangular yard for the kids' swing set and sandbox and bikes; Earl maintains a strict edge on three sides, a six-foot privacy fence across the back between their house and Galen and Vivian's. I have to admit, it's pleasant here.

Emily and Earl's youngest child, five-year-old Evan, is playing with his five-year-old nephew in the sand-box in the back corner of the yard, their "vrooms" and giggles providing a sweet distraction. When I got Emily's bemused email six years ago telling me she and Earl were expecting their seventh child in the same month their first grandchild was due, I dared to hope we might be spared another E name, but no such luck. Oh, there are plenty more, she wrote breezily, and now she's pregnant with their eighth. I shudder to think what we're in store for this time. Eurydice. Epiphany. Elvis—could I love a nephew named Elvis? Or maybe, with simple elegance, Eight.

"But if the memories are repressed, or if it happened when you were pre-verbal—"

"Emily. Give it up. That's not what this is about."

The little boys' chatter suddenly turns hostile. By the time I'm aware of the change, Emily is on her way to the sandbox, hands on hipbones to balance the weight of her belly.

Observing her expert mediation, I miss my own family acutely. Today is Tuesday. Tara has a swimming lesson this afternoon. Martin will get her there. He's an attentive, reliable father. It's just a swimming lesson, but I feel left out, sorrowful.

"That story you sent me," Emily says when she's settled in the wicker rocker again. For some reason, she doesn't look at me.

I hardly remember sending her a story, can't imagine now why I would have done so, and fervently wish I hadn't. "That was a long time ago. God, Em, it must have been in college. These days my writing is all for work." I've lied to my family all my life, so there's no good reason for me to feel guilty about it now. "Which story was it?"

"It was about incest."

"It was fiction, not autobiography." In a sense, everything a writer writes is autobiographical, of course, but Emily's not likely to know that.

Coyly, she asks, "In a sense, everything's autobiographical, isn't it?"

"Not in that sense."

"I still have that story."

"Really?" That pleases me inordinately, and gives me pause. I would like to ask if our father read it, too.

"How come you've never sent me any more?"

"All I write these days are reports and memos."

"That's too bad."

"Highly *creative* reports and memos, mind you."

She giggles. I chuckle. Our laughter doesn't take off this time and I'm disappointed.

What are my daughters conversing about? I have never bothered to disabuse Alexandra of the suspicion, useful to a single father raising an oppositional child, that I could read her mind; at some level she still half-believes this misinterpretation. Emily, on the other hand, most likely does not regard me as having any particular power at all, a perspective that also misses the point.

Standing in thin shade just beyond the edge of the space Emily and Earl have claimed for their unadorned yard, I keep myself hidden from them without much effort. I doubt either of them can feel me watching, or has any inkling of what I intend to do. Maybe not today, but someday soon.

Maybe today.

"Hey, Will."

Tall and stocky, golden hair lightened and sheened by grey streaks and by the diffuse sunlight through all those trees, our brother Will comes bearing gifts:

a little blue bowl two-thirds full of lettuce in various shades of green, orange carrots, pale green cucumber slices with dark green rims, early red tomatoes. I'm swept by regret that we've drifted apart—rushed apart, been catapulted apart; once I left home, we both decided to have absolutely nothing in common anymore. But he's my brother, and I'm so glad to see him.

Will brings a salad made from his home-grown vegetables. Later in the season it will be beans, squash, pumpkins, none of them good enough for Will. Behind him, affecting a stringent indifference, Carol has roses for the table. She does not do any gardening. Neither do their children, beyond occasional mowing under duress. They defend themselves from Will's anxiety about gardening by having nothing to do with it, and I am surprised she deigns even to carry the vase. The roses are pretty, though by no means beautiful.

Alone among my children, Will used to help me in the garden. It was always a struggle. He never had the knack. Then as now, he sensed my intention for him to learn gardening from me, but misinterpreted it, believed he would be carrying on generation after generation some sort of vital family tradition, like taking over the family Christmas when I could not do it anymore or adding himself onto the family business: "Kove and Son." I am supposed to be pleased. I am supposed to praise him. I am supposed to be proud.

Never mind that I gave up labouring in the garden a long time ago, once I learned how to accept what the grocery stores and the wood had to offer. Never mind that I do not even like lettuce. Will's fundamental limitation is that he does not pay attention. I see what gardening means to him, and I find it vastly annoying; he has concocted the significance of it and then proceeded to torture himself and everybody else with his own neurotic fantasy. What I wanted was for him to have a passion whose products would make the world a better place, and gardening seemed for Will the best possibility. In his hands, gardening has added more to the sum of the world's unease than to its bounty.

"All you'd have to do," instructs Emily, whose own burden and raison d'être is that of procreator and family manager, "is walk around his garden with him once in a while and tell him how nice it looks. Comment on his flowers and vegetables. Come on, Dad, how hard is that?"

Impossible, is what it is. Too much and too little is at stake. I know very well what he needs from me; I gave him that need, inserted it in him as deliberately as if I had removed the top of his skull, dumped it in, stirred things around, and replaced the lid. At times, when I despise myself in general, this seems to have been a particularly egregious cruelty, and I suspect I may have had no motive more honourable than the impulse to populate my world with familiars.

I know precisely what he needs. Better than he does, better than Emily does, I know what Will needs. And I cannot spare it. He demands it in a more and more concentrated form. For years now, the best this son and I can do is avoid each other's gaze.

From off in the woods, well outside the parameters of Emily's yard, a four-note song makes itself known. I have the sense that it's been going on for some time and I've only now become aware of it. My skin crawls in appreciation of its eerie beauty. It isn't a birdcall. "What *is* that?"

"What is what?"

"That—music." She looks at me blankly. The four notes come again. "There! Hear it?"

"Oh, that's Vaughn playing his didgeridoo."

"Every time I hear him, it sounds different and I don't know what it is."

"That's Vaughn in a nutshell."

Will and Carol have pulled up chairs beside us now. "How ya doing, Sis?" Will greets me. "Emily filling you in on what's been happening in the family?"

"Maybe you can fill me in, too." For some reason, it seems a daring thing to say. Will snorts.

"So, William, how does your garden grow?" Smiling sweetly and resting her chin on her hand, Emily makes no attempt to disguise the fact that this is meant as a barb—though, given their childhood patterns, if called on it I bet she'd claim she was sincerely inquiring or, at worst, only teasing. I don't know what's going on here. I'm wary. But I'm also sister to both of them, and it's age-old fun to see them fight.

Carol, however, has no such interest; she rolls her eyes and gets up to go talk to Galen's new wife Vivian. I wonder what it's like to be an in-law in this family.

True to form, Will rises to the bait, sounding about twelve years old. "Shut up, Emily."

Merrily she sings out, "Did you ever think that maybe gardening just isn't your thing? Some people have a green thumb and some don't, you know?"

This makes him downright truculent. "When's the last time *you* grew anything?" Instantly realizing his gaffe, he flushes. Emily doesn't let him off the hook. She pats her belly with both hands and gives him a beatific smile. He mutters, "Shit."

She doesn't give it up. "I almost called you the other day. On public television this guy said you can make a fertilizer and pesticide all in one out of stuff like chewing tobacco and beer and mouthwash. Maybe you ought to try that."

Will glowers at her, and I see he's seriously upset. "Johnny Arentzen, Master Gardener. I used to watch him all the time. I tried all that stuff."

"And it didn't work?" She knows it didn't work. What's she doing? "So is he a charlatan? The Jim Bakker of gardening?"

When Will glances at me and away again, I realize Emily's performing, and provoking him to perform, for my benefit. Will gets up and growls over his shoulder as he stomps into the house, "Nothing works."

Sitting back in the fat wicker chair as much as her belly will allow, Emily chortles. "Amazing. Absolutely amazing."

"What was that all about?"

"Will's got some sort of weird neurosis about gardening."

I say as mildly as I can, "I don't think I've ever heard of a gardening neurosis."

"You know how people use horticulture as therapy? Well, big brother Will needs therapy *because* of horticulture." She laughs.

"Probably doesn't help to tease him about it, then."

"Oh, I know. I'm bad. But it's so much fun! He's always been such an easy mark."

I have nearly filled my pouch with poisonous plants of a remarkable variety, some of which alter the consciousness, some only kill. This is enough for today. I start to re-enter the family gathering in Emily's neat yard, then stop short. With so many people around, so many small children, the contents of the pouch must not be here. Glad for an excuse to escape, I set off through the yellow wood toward my house.

The four notes repeat, and then segue into a long, complicated musical phrase, which repeats and then segues into another. Discovering I'm holding my breath, I try to exhale without being obvious about it. "Does he do this often?"

"More and more." She smiles and shakes her head. "More and more."

Vaughn is filling the woods with exquisite, heart-breaking music. Music separates man from lesser beasts, one of the few things I would call "holy." I have no musical talent. I found and developed it in him. The Kove family will bring good into this world.

Emily asks me out of the blue, "Remember how Mom used to play the harmonica?"

"The *harmonica?* Mom?" I can't imagine why I'm so outraged. "That was Dad."

"Mom used to go out into the woods at dusk and not come back until we were all in bed. Sometimes I could hear her harmonica. She only knew a few songs. 'Old Black Joe.' 'Red River Valley.'"

"You're wrong, Em. How could you remember something like that anyway? You were only three years old when she left. Do you really remember anything about her?"

Hands on belly, my little sister glances at me and then away, and I think how much time and effort our family puts into not looking at each other. I think of Martin's direct brown gaze and am faint with homesickness. Emily says grimly, "I used to think I could remember how she smelled, but I don't think so anymore."

"Oh," I breathe, "Em," and I reach for her hand, but she's heaved herself up out of the chair to join one of her young-adult daughters—the tall one; Erin, I think—who is pushing little kids on the swings.

There's a story in this. Music from the woods. Primal memories that may or may not be factual but are certainly true. Gardening as a metaphor and concentrate for despair. Far from diminishing the importance and immediacy of an experience, writing gives me a way in. I'm sipping my lemonade and considering various opening images when several people suddenly and simultaneously demand, "Where's Dad? Where's Grandpa? Has anybody seen Daddy?" A Kove family Greek chorus, commenting on the action and sounding an alarm.

The instant I set foot in the woods, I'd be lost, or might as well be. And, of course, as long as I'm here, I'm always in the woods. The whole point of Emily's careful yard is that it's cut out of the woods. Will's garden is defined by being not-woods; he bitches about the volunteer trees he has to keep digging out because, since he doesn't want them there, they're weeds. Around Galen's house is a ludicrous six-foot privacy fence, reportedly Vivian's idea. I can't say that I blame her. Around Vaughn's cabin is a patch of cleared and trampled ground that makes me imagine him pacing and dancing. There's virtually no boundary between my father's house, the yellow house I grew up in, and the yellow woods.

"I'd get lost myself."

Will and Galen look at me with contempt. It's all I can do not to stick my tongue out at them. Emily pats my hand. "You just stay here with me, Sandi. It's not the first time he's wandered off."

But alarm pervades the family gathering now, and Emily's alarmed, too. At least I think she is; my sister is enough of a stranger to me that I don't have a baseline against which to judge her reactions. Her eyes keep darting to the woods all around us; I couldn't swear that she doesn't always do this, but I haven't noticed it before, and I can't stop my gaze from following hers, over the fence to the woods on the north, on the south, on the east, back toward the house on the other side of which we both know the woods spreads yellow and familiar and mysterious. Our father is somewhere out there.

The crowd has thinned considerably. Earl stays at the grill, and Emily doesn't go beyond the edge of the yard, even that much movement causing her to pant visibly and brace her lower back with her hands. The youngest kids haven't left, though they seem distracted in their play; Evan goes to his mother and insists she hold him, which in order to do she has to make her ponderous way back toward me to a vacated lawn chair. Most of the older kids and all the other adults have gone looking for the missing patriarch, a search party that doesn't seem entirely impromptu. I imagine them fanning out through the woods, each in an assigned, practised position.

"Where does he usually go?"

"He always comes back on his own. Everybody goes out searching and when they give up he's at his house as if nothing ever happened."

"Another bit of Kove family performance art."

"What's that supposed to mean?"

At times since I've been here she'd have known what I meant. We'd have shared a supercilious chuckle at the eccentricities of our family. I don't know why she's pissed off now, and I don't much care. The kids have gotten a Frisbee stuck in a tree and I hurry to help retrieve it, then offhandedly tell the kids I'm going for a walk. They may or may not relay the message to anybody who cares.

By the time I get to the gate, irritation with my crazy family is close to revulsion, and I intend to put as much distance as possible between them and me without actually leaving and going home. The fact that I can't go home quite yet infuriates me, and as I plunge into the woods I break branches, crush flowers, disturb tiny lairs, look for webs to destroy, and make no attempt to avoid the snake that flows alongside me for a few steps. The snake, however, avoids me, proving how much better it fits into this world than I ever will.

Chapter 5

Pa left the Old Country when he was seventeen. This is my tale of origin, scanty as it is and begging for embellishment.

Once I overheard my sister telling her granddaughter he was twenty-two. When I confronted her she insisted he had told her that. She had it confused, or she had some arcane reason for lying. This was between my sister and me until the day she died; indeed, I still hold it against her.

Pa did not lie, and he always told me seventeen. There is no written proof of this or of much else. Family records are skeletal and so open to interpretation they are apocryphal, more metaphor than history.

Sometimes as I put one foot in front of the other to get through the day, I indulge myself in imagining legends that might grow up around the facts of what I am doing here and now:

"Every morning he used to walk to the fork in the path and turn around and around to all four directions."

"Half of what we ate when we were kids he harvested from the woods. And remedies, and potions, and dyes. And toys: bendable stems you could braid into rings, leaves that looked like stars, roots that we dressed up like ugly little dolls."

"He planted things in the woods. See that big tree over there? These tiny little flowers you can't find unless you already know where to look, and even then sometimes not? He planted those. That plant with the fuzzy leaves, too, and that purplish one. Be careful. They're poisonous. Yes, they are. He told me so."

In this way, getting through the day is made to mean both more and less than it literally does. Sometimes, contemplation of my legacy lengthens my stride and directs my gaze. Sometimes, distracted, I stumble.

I do have the copy of Pa's obituary that my sister clipped. Why we should need such a memento is beyond me. I would not have saved it. I conspicuously did not look for it in the paper at the time of his death, and certainly have never read and re-read it as she did, smoothing its folds, weeping and smiling. But once it came into my possession, throwing it away seemed, though I am not a religious man, sacrilegious. And it is, after all, proof of something—proof that my father lived and now is dead, proof that I am an orphan, a ludicrous concept for a man my age.

Knowing no one outside his village, Pa—no one's father yet—came on a boat to America with very little money, *very little English, few job skills, and only the most amorphous and idealized intention of finding a better life. He made his way, more or less. I have no way of knowing whether, when all was said and done, he was glad to have come here, worked in the steel mills of the Monongahela Valley, bought the tall thin house on Pearl Street, married the saintly Julia and then the wicked Mary. Had children. Had grandchildren. Had me. I do not know whether it turned out to be a better life.*

He lived to be seventy-eight, an age I meant to note and did not when I passed it myself a few years ago. He dropped dead of a heart attack on the steps of the doctor's office where he had just been pronounced hale. By then he had long lost all touch with the Old Country except for his habitual reversal of v's and w's, an American surname with a Slovak tinge, the fruit-filled Christmas cookies he taught my sister and my wife to make (Emily's version can best be said to have been loosely inspired by the original), and a set of three minimalist stories:

1. He told me the river teemed with fish. He never gave details, I never asked for any, but my hungry imagination supplied: thick as cream, silver and iridescent blue, with a gushing odour I could only think to call fishy. He said that in spring the villagers, the boy who would be my father among them, waded out into the swollen river with wide sleeves billowing, netting multitudes of fish. Imagining slimy squirming against bare upper arms, I would shudder and rub my own flesh. As new words entered my vocabulary I applied them to this story: freshet, spawn.

2. My father's family—my family, though I have never succeeded in feeling part of the line—lived in a big stone house, one blocky grey-and-white photograph of which is still extant. When Pa was small, he told me, a fire destroyed most of the wooden houses in the village and everyone moved into his house. As I learned them, I ascribed to this story the words community and neighbourliness, invasion and melee, generosity and obligation.

3. Pa's mother, my grandmother whom I never knew and therefore have no name for other than the given name Maria, which I cannot help pronouncing with an American accent, gave him a gift to take with him into the New World. My sister told her granddaughter it was his aunt, but Pa told me it was his mother and Pa did not lie. Packaged and discrete as an heirloom, consciously given and received, the gift was the courage to break her heart by leaving the big sheltering stone house when they both knew he would never come back. Every time he recounted this story, which I alone must have heard a hundred times, Pa's eyes filled. She held him by the shoulders to bestow her blessing on him: "Go, son. I would go with you if I could. God help me, I would go instead of you. But I'm afraid." She shook him, he said. She kissed him. "Go anyway, son. Be brave for us both."

"I'm not brave," he said he told her. "I'm afraid."

"It isn't bravery if you aren't afraid." Like his mother's name, this adage must have sounded quite different in

the language of my father's youth, which he made a point
not to pass down.

Only three anecdotes. Not nearly enough. Despite the
personal cost, I have offered my children far more than
that. They have as many stories about my life as I could
find for them. It is probably not nearly enough, either. Or
perhaps it is far too much.

"What *is* that?"

"That's Vaughn banging on his goddamn drum."

"Why?"

"Because Vaughn is Vaughn. Maybe he thinks Dad'll
hear it and find his way home. Maybe it has nothing to do with Dad. How the hell should I know why
Vaughn does anything?"

"Does Daddy actually get lost?" It's hard for me to
imagine our father at risk in these familiar woods,
except from his own plans and potions, which I have
still not mentioned to any of my siblings. But the
alarm of my sister and brothers and several of their
children is contagious.

"There's no telling what he'll do, either." Galen has
always regarded our family as a bunch of loonies,
himself the lone exception. He's got a point, though
getting married at his age was a surprise—from
him, downright weird. Right now he seems more
irritated than anything else. But then, that's always
been the distinguishing characteristic of my oldest

brother. Everything irritates him. Life irritates him. He approves of nothing and nobody. No matter what the situation, it's never good enough for him. I suppose this chronic dissatisfaction comes in handy for a habitual social activist, but on a personal level it's a pain in the ass. Rather savagely I wonder how Vivian stands him, what possessed her to marry him.

He's been irritated with me all my life. Since he picked me up at the airport a month ago, he's hardly made an attempt to uncurl his lip. At the moment he's close to furious, and as I did so many times in our shared distant past, I rise to the bait.

At his heels as we crash through the yellow underbrush, I demand, "You've never much liked me, have you, Galen?"

He snorts, doesn't turn or pause. "For Chrissake, Alexandra, this isn't about you. I know it's hard to believe, but not everything is about you."

I'm out of practice. "Shut up," is the best I can come up with.

Behind me, Will snaps, "Will you two knock it off?" And there we are again, all in our places: Galen and I bickering, Will struggling to keep the peace, Emily worrying and directing from home, Vaughn off somewhere doing his own eccentric version of the current family activity, and all of it spun off from and looping back to Daddy, the source and the inspiration, the seed of the pearl or the source of the infection depending on your point of view.

We trudge. Every once in a while one of us calls one of our various names for him—"Daddy!" "Dad!" "Alexander Kove!"—but from our father there's no response any of us can hear. Birds screech and there are startled rustlings and thumps, Vaughn's drum among them, not far away. These woods are inhabited. The space they form is a container with a tight lid out of which I crawled a long time ago, from which I've never escaped, which I've never fully explored though I spent hours and days and nights of my childhood within it.

We're walking fast, listening hard, each of us searching for our father. "Do we have a plan here or are we just sort of flailing?"

Galen doesn't deign to answer. After a moment, Will says, "He has a hideout he goes to sometimes when the family gets to be too much for him."

For reasons I don't pretend to understand, I don't admit to already knowing this. With careful obfuscation just this side of an outright lie, I express my incredulity, which in itself is sincere. "A hideout? He's eighty-fucking-one years old."

Contemptuously, Galen corrects me. "Eighty-fucking-two."

"Sorry."

"Yeah, well, you've missed a few birthdays."

Pointedly I speak to Will, not to Galen. That'll show

him. "Like the hideout he had as a kid to get away from the wicked stepmother."

"What are you talking about?"

"His stepmother Mary used to chase him with a butcher knife or a fireplace poker and he'd hide in a hollowed-out place in the hedge that divided their yard from the Petrovskys'. Remember?"

"Who?"

"The next-door neighbours. John and what was her name? Ida?"

"John and Irena Petrovsky. Their sons were Bill and Les. But I never heard that hideout story." Will seems not so much sceptical as wary.

Galen is firmer. "That's not one of Dad's stories. You're making that up."

Panic skitters in me like Vaughn's drumbeat. "Oh, come on, you guys. He used to show us the spot in the hedge every time we'd visit Grandpa. He wouldn't let us play in there. Remember?"

"Hey, Alexandra, I thought you weren't into fiction anymore."

"Sandi. Her name is Sandi now."

Ahead of me and behind me on the narrow path, my brothers chortle and, predictably, I yell at them. "What's so funny, assholes?"

"Ooh," Galen turns to sneer. "She's getting mad."

Will volleys the ridicule back past my head. "Ooh. I'm scared."

"Fuck you!"

They laugh outright, and I am swept by the ancient murderous rage I haven't felt since I left this place and these people. Though Martin and I occasionally find each other thunderously frustrating, we've made it a point to fight fair. Even my children, whose early survival depended on their ability to read people and whose skill at driving me crazy can be impressive, don't get to me like this.

"Fuck you!" I shriek again, a trapped and powerless adolescent fighting for my life again and revelling in it. "I don't need this!"

Storming off the path into the tangled yellow wood is so intensely gratifying I don't care how reckless it might be. Shouting for my father is a cover; I'm not really looking for him anymore. My brothers don't follow or even call me back. They just go on without me.

Taking the shortcut is like blazing a trail through the wood every time, although I come this way often and I suspect others do as well—Vaughn routinely and some of my grandchildren once in a while. Over- and undergrowth move in with an energy and speed that can seem magical and directed but is nothing more or less than their nature, filling in footprints and healing broken branches or, more likely, forcing them altogether out of existence. I always travel the same route, and these woods are not very deep.

Even so, today I have become anxious and contemptibly unsure of myself.

To entice my children from one place to another through the wood, I used games. Treasure hunts: I would hide pennies, many of which are probably still here, camouflaged now as dirt and leaves; as the children got older, it had to be at least quarters, and once in a while, just to keep things interesting, I would plant a dollar bill or two, which really did look and feel a bit like foliage. Scavenger hunts with lists whose ulterior purpose was to improve vocabulary and encourage abstract thought:

A variegated leaf.

Two objects that, taken together, could be said to form a sequence.

Something secret.

Something powerful.

A gift.

Alexandra once brought home two bits of trash, a broken crayon, and part of a brown paper bag, with and on which she wrote me a little poem about a grasshopper and claimed it met the criteria for the last three items—a secret and powerful gift. Her sister and brothers objected on grounds that she had not found the poem but made it. I had to rule with them, and Alexandra did not win the prize, but I thought she understood my pride in her. More than that, I thought she was signalling that she understood what was happening between us, what

88

I was trying to pass along to her and what she would do with it when it was her own. As it has turned out, I was wrong.

A red fox has a den somewhere around here. I move carefully. Vaughn's drum has stopped, or sunk beneath my auditory threshold. This little blue spruce seems to me not to have grown an inch in height or girth in all the years I have been passing by it, though it looks perfectly healthy, round as a snowman, needle tips blue as the pale blue sky.

My children would have me stay out of the wood. Emily says flat out that I am getting too old for this. It is true that my knees hurt and buckle from the slightest jar. Many days I have barely enough strength in my arms to push low-hanging branches and cottony spider webs out of the way. It is also true that my ability to control myself and the world is less and less reliable. As often as not now, I end up somewhere I had not planned to go. But then, I often end up somewhere I had not planned to go whether I am in the wood or not.

Vaughn's drum has stopped. This seems as weird to me as the fact that he was walking through the woods playing it in the first place. His studied eccentricity is already wearing thin. I resent how my attention has swung to him, exactly what he wants, and the shudder of alarm and anticipation that makes me stumble and veer.

An animal crosses the path up ahead as if there were no path, red-gold in shadow and sunlight, and with something like pain I'm thinking of the Hopkins poem about dappled things. That's not one Daddy taught me. I wonder if he knows it, or if I might teach it to him.

I want to be thinking about the family I have chosen and constructed for myself rather than my family of, as they say, origin. But it's hard to keep my mind on them. I miss them in the same pervasive, tissue-deep way I'd notice having not enough air to breathe.

The first time we saw Tara, the traumatized six-year-old with a history we didn't share who would be our miraculous daughter, she was crouched on the floor in the living room of the foster home, fingering puzzle pieces without much apparent attempt to fit them together. Skilfully, she was not acknowledging us—not looking up, not saying "hi," ignoring our offerings of an elephant puppet and the pictures of what would soon be her house. The foster mother kept apologizing for Tara's "rudeness," insisting she'd taught her better than that. I sat on the floor beside the child, took up a piece of sky, found another to fit into it and make a corner. Tara scooted back away from me, but she was interested. Martin came and just sat with her, not trying for a response, just offering himself. Before we left that first day, she was calling us Mommy and Daddy. I remember how green her eyes were, sheened behind those short dark lashes; her eyes are still astonishing, flashing with defiance or insight, yearning for her father's approval which he seldom openly bestows, curtained against me even when we sit together in the early morning kitchen. I remember the burnt umber of her hand against the beige of mine that first day, how small she was, how thoroughly mine already. She still holds my hand sometimes. If she were here with me now she might be holding my hand. She still calls me Mommy.

The first time we met Ramon, the hurt and angry ten-year-old stranger who would be our beloved son, he didn't want to let us go. His whole taut, pudgy little body said, "You won't come back," and when we did, when we kept coming back, his own relief infuriated him. If he were here with me now, I'd be hunting for him in the yellow woods, and when I found him I'd yell at him and take him in my arms, nearly a man now, taller than I am, yelling back at me and then bending to rest his head on my shoulder.

Off to my left a bird calls oddly. When it repeats I realize it's a musical instrument, some sort of flute—doubtless my peculiar brother Vaughn again. Seriously pissed off now, I crash through prickly undergrowth toward the sound, which is moving. Vaughn may not think he's signalling me, but I have some say in that, too.

Vaughn is in my way. He has been circling me all afternoon. His ubiquitous music could hardly be more dissonant; this is a place for natural sounds, birdcalls and the rattle of branches and wind so high as to be perceptible only by the single sense of hearing. Imposed sounds of poorly played flutes and drums and, God help us, didgeridoos do not belong here—although a case could be made that any sounds any of us makes are by definition natural, because we make them. This is an irritating thought.

Vaughn has been circling me in one way or another since he was fourteen or fifteen years old when first I and then he realized he was homosexual. When I look at him, when I think of him, the nauseating images of my son fellating and sodomizing another man superimpose themselves on everything else. I recognize this as bigotry. I blame Vaughn for asking too much of me and thereby exposing one of my core character traits: hypocrisy arising out of moral turpitude, the spirit being willing but the psyche weak.

There he is, standing in front of me, just barely far enough away to be a silhouette against a pale blue fissure of sky between trees. With various musical instruments attached to his back, belt, wrists, head, neck, ankles, he cuts a foolish figure, a caricature of a minstrel, a ragtag one-man band. His hair fluffs out around a shimmering bald spot. His elbows jump in a rhythm that escapes me. His dancing feet swish through the layers of leaf duff on which we are both standing. He says cheerily, "Listen to this, Dad," and launches into a tune of, I presume, his own composition.

Actually, it is rather good. I cannot stop myself from turning away.

And I am lost.

I have never been here before.

No one knows where I am. Including me.

Something slithers between my feet. It crosses in front of me, coils around me, approaches me from behind and from the side. A snake. My skin crawls as the snake crawls.

"I do not need your help. When I need your help, I will let you know."

Herpie ignores me. If a snake can be said to have ideas, she has ideas of her own. In a patch of sun on a lichen-spotted rock she makes a thin tower of herself, like a child's stacking toy, and from among the coils flicks out her tongue, presumably gathering data I may or may not be interested in using.

I see, though, that I have come to the place I think I intended to reach when I set out on this jaunt, and I suppose Herpie was my guide. That is, after all, her function. I am tempted to say her raison d'être, but I acknowledge, somewhat grudgingly, that probably she has reasons for being besides keeping me from getting lost. I thank her, though. Of course she does not respond. She is a snake.

I must have been about seven, just barely still fitting under the sofa pillow roof inside the sofa pillow walls of my hideout in the corner of the living room, which gave the illusion of hiding me without really doing so; anybody who'd wanted to could have found me. Mama could have found me, but by then we'd had one round of birthdays, one Christmas, one summer, and parts of two school years without her.

From inside the pseudo-shelter of the pillows, I couldn't see or smell or touch Daddy, but I could feel him over there in his big chair, where on Saturday mornings I sat with him and we read to each other and he made me memorize poetry. "Sailed off in a wooden shoe." "Sturdy and staunch he stands." "Admiring bog." "Ghostly galleon." "Come live with me and be my love." "And all but cry with colour!" "The ends of being." "Nevermore!" Nobody else had to do that. They all got to go outside and play in the woods, or they had to do chores, or they'd be at some activity. Me, I sat with Daddy and we read to each other and he made me memorize poetry. "One could do worse." "Say I'm growing old."

This wasn't a Saturday morning. It was evening, winter; I remember how cozy it was inside my pillow hideout inside our house inside our woods, which couldn't have been yellow at that time of year but always *felt* yellow. On Daddy's big white console radio, people were talking. I wasn't paying attention to the words, just their voices, serious, important, giving me a sense that there were important things to know in the world and I could know them.

Daddy's recliner was creaking a little; the mere thought of his thin black-stockinged feet up in the air made me feel privileged and terribly responsible. Probably he had one of his headaches. I was afraid of his headaches and resented him for them. He was my Daddy. He could get rid of his headaches if he wanted to. If he loved me enough. My brothers and sister weren't around. I don't know where they were.

All of a sudden, whole and clear and pure as a trumpet, one man on the radio was saying, "Homosexuality is unnatural," and the other man was countering, "Handkerchiefs aren't natural, either. That groove in your upper lip is so the mucus from your nose can run straight into your mouth."

I was seven. Bodily functions were of tremendous interest. The man on the radio couldn't have picked a more persuasive metaphor. Now I find his implication that being gay is more civilized than being straight a bit much, but at the time it was nothing short of an epiphany, a palpable shift in the way I looked at things, a sudden breakthrough into profound tolerance. It also instilled in me, all of a piece, a reverence for the power of words.

"Did you hear that, Alexandra?" came my father's quiet query. Naturally, he'd known where I was all along. "I want you to remember that. Do you understand?" Choked with wonder, I could only nod. He couldn't have seen me inside the pillow house, but he said to me softly, just between us, "Good girl," and in that instant words became associated with my father's power over me and mine over him, with neither of which I have yet come to terms.

Vaughn has launched into a song, probably one he's making up on the spot, or maybe something inspired by whatever man is his current lover and muse. It's not bad. It draws me in. Now I want to find him a lot more than I want to find our father. Calling his name a couple of times produces no results. When I come upon a branch shaped like the seat of a chair, which I'm not sure whether I remember or not though it must have been here when I was a kid, I settle myself onto it. It gives under my weight and there's nothing to brace myself, but it doesn't break.

A memory surfaces. About five years old, I was playing at being lost in the woods. When somebody found me or I got tired and went home on my own I would be in big trouble, but it would have been worth it. I could hear the music Daddy made on his harmonica, so I wasn't alone, and even if I didn't know where I was or where I was going, there was always the sense of having a guide.

I didn't round a bend in the path or crest a hill or push through a thicket or anything; from my childish

96

perspective, Daddy just materialized. Much later, when I learned about gargoyles and gnomes, I would flash to how he looked: shadowed in a little cave under an overhanging rock, crouching around the magical instrument in his hands, eyes on me.

Then the keening music stopped—to me it seemed in the middle of the song, but knowing my father's characteristic neatness, it probably wasn't. He lowered his cupped hands. "Alexandra," he said. "Come here. I have something to show you."

I remember hoping my brothers would show up and just as desperately hoping they wouldn't. Where were they, anyway? The woods were still and might as well have been home to nothing but me and Daddy.

"Come over here, Alexandra." This time it was a command, though not yet harsh. For a long time, much of what I did was to get him to say my name like that.

Taking several steps toward him, I could see what he held. Not the harmonica, though I hadn't noticed him put it down, but a lump the size of a basketball of some thick squishy substance like modelling clay. There was a face in it. I looked again. There were three, four, six, countless faces in it, under my father's hands.

But then, with a chill, I saw that he wasn't touching the clay. His hands made a place for it, but there was space all around between the surface of the brown lump and his long white hands. The faces were taking and losing shape into and out of the clay, all by themselves. Except that I knew he had something to do with it. He had something to do with everything.

I sat down on the ground beside him and together we watched the cavalcade of faces emerge and recede. Daddy told me who they were. Not anybody we knew personally, but people who, Daddy gave me to understand, were real and lived in this world. People of all different races. Having never seen anybody who wasn't white, I found them beautiful and hideous, alluring and scary. Old people, even older than Grandpa, whom we saw once a year. Newborns and not-even newborns with only the promise of faces; right there and then he made me memorize the pronunciation and spelling of the new words: foetus; embryo. People with no arms, blind people, people who couldn't walk. All kinds of people in that ball of clay. I stared.

Then my father took my hands. Took them for his own. Daddy touched us often and easily so there was nothing alarming about that, but when I guessed his intention I recoiled and squirmed and tried to close my fists. He was stronger and smarter than I would ever be. His long, thin fingers dwarfed mine. His palms were twice the size of the backs of my hands.

With great care he positioned my hands where he wanted them among all those faces, and then he pressed down. The clay gave, shifted, rose between my fingers and around my wrists. It was neither warm nor cool, neither wet nor dry. It felt just like me. I couldn't tell where my flesh ended and the flesh of all those faces began.

My father held me there. With his arms around me from behind, I felt his breathing and his heartbeat through my shoulder blades. His thin thighs in those silly plaid pants made a V that I fit right into, protecting my back while exposing me to whatever came next.

The faces were moving. I felt eyes open and close, mouths turn up and down, brows knit; my own eyes, mouth, eyebrows, cheeks, teeth, tongue, chin slid into one expression after another. My left thumb quivered from the pulse under someone's jaw, and my own pulse raced. A moustache rasped the web between my right ring finger and pinky, and the skin of my own upper lip prickled. The insides of my wrists were tickled by hair quite unlike my own—nappy, luxuriant, sparse, stiff—and the roots of my braids stirred.

At five years old, I understood without thinking about it that magic existed in the world in much the same way as weather or the woods: perfectly natural by definition, since it was part of everyday life and by nature mysterious. When later I could put words to what transpired that morning, it came as no surprise that Daddy had been giving me both a gift and an order, neither of which I had the option to refuse, even if I'd wanted to, which at that point I didn't.

Personally, Daddy didn't like people who were different from him. His discomfort around my best friend Penny was mortifying, and he outright glowered at my Korean homecoming date, whom I'd had to go into the city to find. Later the next day, my father had the balls to say to me, "I taught you wrong."

"Daddy is a traitor, Daddy is a prick. Daddy is a hypocrite, Daddy is a dick."

I am sitting on the ground. I have no memory of having sat down, so the change in position feels magical, even sinister, although it probably is neither. I am in a familiar place. I am in the grotto I have both found and fashioned under the overhang of this rock slab protruding from this hill. In order to enter, one must crawl; therefore, I must have crawled.

I conduct my standard inventory, among simultaneous sensations that I have never done this before and that I did so only a few moments ago. Nothing seems to be missing: books, notebooks, granola bars, bottled water, flashlight, various potions, various poisons, raw ingredients for both. I have use for them all.

Vaughn comes ambling toward me. At the moment he's not actually playing any instrument, but he's festooned like a Christmas tree with all manner of objects that rattle and swish and clang in rhythm as he moves. For a moment he seems not to notice me, and I'm ready to be pissed, but then he does stop. "Fancy meeting you here," and he salutes me.

"Hey, Vaughn. I've been enjoying your music."

"Thanks." He ducks his head.

"Have you seen Daddy?"

"He's in his hideout."

"Where's that?"

"Over that way." He gestures unhelpfully.

When I start to get up, the branch creaks, so I ease myself back down to say cautiously, "Music is really important to you, isn't it?"

"It's what I do." When he shrugs, something thin and metallic rings. "It's Daddy it's important to."

"But you like it," I persist. "You love it. Right? You love music. That's why you play it all the time."

"I hate music."

"You're not serious." For answer, I suppose, or elaboration, or just because he feels like it, he pounds his fist half a dozen times on the snare drum strapped around his waist, making an awful racket. "No, you don't," I splutter stupidly. "Nobody hates music."

Vaughn raises his flute, folds his lips in, and produces a long *coo* that ends in a screech. "Music makes my ears hurt and my head hurt. Music makes the voices worse."

"Voices? You hear voices?"

"Singing." He grins. "That figures, right?"

"But, Vaughn, your music is beautiful."

"I guess. It's all just noise to me."

"Then why do you do it?"

"I don't have any choice. It's who I am. He gave it to me."

The branch breaks under me. It's a short fall, but jarring, and embarrassing. Vaughn reaches to help me and I manage to get to my feet and turn to survey the damage. I've destroyed the tree seat, part of this landscape for who knows how long. Now there's just a wound in the bark of the trunk and a vaguely oval piece of wood sticking out of the underbrush. "Shit."

"You okay?"

"Yeah." No need to mention that my coccyx aches. "Aside from feeling like a bull in a china shop. A cow in a china shop."

My brother gives me a quick, startling hug and continues on his way, musical no matter what he might have wanted his way to be. I hear him for a long time and find myself walking, breathing, searching for our father to the rhythm he establishes.

I'm not even sure I'm searching for Daddy anymore. There's no chance in hell I could find my way to his hideout again. Maybe he's gone away to die. There would be some sense to that, some rightness and justice that could be called poetic. But I can't stand the thought of it. I quicken my pace, stumble, grab for a branch, break it and savagely break it again. When I shout, "Goddammit, Daddy! Where are you?" my voice is the same voice I've always used with him, thin and petulant, almost immediately absorbed by the yellow woods. The thought of Vaughn possessed not by his own passion for music but by Daddy's—by Daddy's conviction that music deserves passion even though he himself can't produce it—makes me want to set this place on fire.

I'll find him if he wants me to find him. If he doesn't, I won't. It's as simple as that. I force a path for myself, plunging and careening, smashing and breaking and tearing things up, as if the woods were my father's heart.

This peanut butter jar is almost full of dead spiders. Small to begin with and containing minuscule quantities of fluid, the bodies quickly dry and pulverize and ultimately take up little space; there are many arachnid sacrifices in this two-pound jar. The contents of the jar are striated, greyish compacted spider dust on the bottom variegating into the more recently alive, brown and black and still distinctly eight-legged layer on top. Every time I check, there is more room again in the jar.

Dozens of empty baby-wipes boxes, plastic with hinged lids—a material benefit to me of Emily's fecundity— hold my drawing, carving, cutting, weaving, mixing, calibrating, measuring tools. One of them contains the harmonica. Emily indulgently saves them for me, thinking it a doddering old man's harmless eccentricity. The necessary process of checking each one of them consumes a fair amount of time, especially as I lose track more than once and must begin again.

I can never be certain, but it appears nothing has been disturbed. If Vaughn has found this place and sometimes appropriates it for his own hiding, as I have long suspected, he has been following the leave-nothing-take-nothing rule of the respectful trespasser.

As I pour one thing into another and stir, I become aware that someone is here. Alexandra is here. I crawl out of the cave to face her down.

"Well, there you are."

My jaw and fists clench almost involuntarily at her condescending tone, and I respond condescendingly, "Yes. Here I am."

"Everybody's looking for you."

"Really? Everybody?"

"Well, Galen and Will. And Vaughn, sort of."

"And you."

For the reply she is tempted to make, she substitutes, "They seemed to think you might be lost or in danger."

"When have I ever been lost in this wood?"

"Don't ask me."

He used to stand at the fork in the path and turn around and around to look in all four directions. He'd bring home ugly little roots my brothers and sister and I would dress up like dolls. He made meals, remedies, dyes, potions out of stuff from the woods. Half of what grows in the woods he planted—big trees, tiny flowers, plants with fuzzy leaves, and purplish plants he sometimes said were poisonous and sometimes insisted were not.

Now he gets to his feet. The planes of his already angular face show their bones. His thin shoulders have squared. His elbows and knees jut belligerently; noticing my father's elbows and knees makes me a little queasy. While he glares at me I lift my chin and hold his gaze, but when he dismisses me, turns his back, starts to move away, I crumble.

"Daddy, wait." He doesn't wait. He never has. But it's the only chance I have. "Ever since I got here I've been trying to read something to you. Can I read it to you now?"

Since the day she was born I have done nothing but wait for Alexandra. I do not intend to wait now just because she tells me to. But she knows how to get to me; at the promise of her reading to me something she has written, against my will I pause. At my right ankle is a needle-leafed flat-headed ground clover whose name has escaped me but whose use I well know.

"Don't laugh at me!" I'm yelling like a thirteen-year-old, furiously insulted, hurt, and invigorated. He doesn't say anything, but he doesn't laugh anymore, either, and in terms of capitulation that's the best I can hope for from him. "Goddammit, you listen. I did this for you."

This is it. This is the moment. This is the reason she came home, and the reason she stayed away. She has written something for me.

But I've been deceived. She has deceived me again, eluded me, refused me again. What she is reading is that damned letter from the Old Country that she tried to show me at Emily's the other day. In awkward English, which she reads awkwardly, it mentions people I do not doubt are family members, descendants of the brothers and sisters Pa left behind. The letter concludes with an invitation for ongoing correspondence and is signed, "Your cousin, Elena."

Alexandra's childlike expectancy is vexing. It is true that, years ago, I might have been gratified; at one time I toyed with the notion of travelling to the village from which my father emigrated and the family he left. Alexandra must have known that. But she has misjudged. She is too late. Somewhat to my satisfaction, I have absolutely no interest now, and no interest in feigning any. "It wasn't easy tracking the family down," she informs me indignantly. "It took a while." *Perhaps I nod. She holds the letter out to me. I do not take it.* "Here. The address is on the envelope."

"I do not write letters."

"You used to. I have a couple of letters you wrote to me."

I wave her off. This time she does nothing to stop me as I push my way along a faint path away from her, but it is a long, uncomfortable time before I am safely out of her field of vision.

He's vanished into the woods now, and I don't give a shit if he's lost or if he takes his own fucking life. It's all his.

By the time I get back to the edge of Emily's yard, I'm shaking with fury and can hardly open the gate. I hear him behind me, and then he reaches around me and opens the gate for me, ushering me in as if he owned the place.

Chapter 6

Babysitting the three younger kids while Emily and Earl are at the hospital having Eight, I enjoy just reciting the names—Eli, Erin, Evan. Imagining that their mother does, too, makes me feel connected to her, which is sort of pitiful when you think about it. The four older ones—Eddie, Elizabeth, Eva, Eileen—all had reasons they couldn't be here. That's fine with me. It suits me to be taking care of my niece and nephews at a time of family need. And there's not a barbecue in sight.

Emily's due date is a full two months away. It was Earl who called me in the middle of the night, waking me from a deep sleep and a complicated dream; not knowing my brother-in-law well, I could only assume this brusqueness to be his crisis mode. Not knowing my little sister very well, either, I asked to talk to her, but Earl said she couldn't come to the phone, which scared me and hurt my feelings. All I wanted to say was good luck and I love you.

Apparently Daddy hadn't been awakened by the phone, or had assumed it was for me and would add the disturbance of his sleep to the list of things he holds against me, such as the fact that I didn't go to the Phi Beta Kappa ceremony in college and get the key he'd paid ten dollars for. I don't know now why I didn't go.

Even before dawn, it was warm enough to sit out here on the deck, and now it's quite comfortable on its way to being too hot. Birds are riotous, countless different calls. If Ramon, our nature-lover, were here, he'd stand in the sunrise with eyes closed and a look of rapture on his handsome face. Homesickness slices through me, a physical pain.

"What'd you do, smother them in their beds?"

"Jesus, Will. I didn't know you were there."

"Sorry. Good morning, Sandi. It's quiet, which can't be said very often about Emily's house."

"Good morning, Will. Nobody's up yet."

"Lucky you."

"What are you doing here?"

"Thought I'd stop by on my way to work to make sure you were okay. It can get a little wild around here."

"So far so good. They're easy when they're not conscious."

"Good thing it's summer. School days are something else. Emily and Earl have it down to a science.

Everybody's assigned fifteen minutes in the bathroom. Not sixteen."

"You know, it never dawned on me until I was a parent myself what it must have been like for Daddy to get all five of us out the door in the morning. I don't remember a lot of chaos or hassle, do you?"

"You girls always hogged the bathroom."

"Until you boys started shaving."

"You and Emily would hole up in there teasing your hair for hours. We'd pound on the door. In junior high I used to wake up every hour all night long worrying about having time to take a shower and brush my teeth." He's grinning, but bitterly.

"Oh, sure. It's my fault you got such lousy grades. Sleep deprivation, right?" I'm grinning, but we're on the brink of a fight.

"When my kids were growing up," he declares icily, "I made sure they had equal time."

Now I'm worrying that I've missed this with my own children, that our basic family routines and arrangements have felt unfair to one or the other or both of them, that they'll carry into adulthood resentment Martin and I never knew about, as my brother obviously has. "Are you in a hurry?" I risk asking him. "Do you have time for a cup of coffee?"

"Sure," he agrees readily, and I'm pleased. He's inside for longer than it would take just to pour a cup of coffee in a familiar kitchen, and I imagine him listening for the kids, maybe checking on them in their various beds. Old habit would have me in a snit that he doesn't trust me. Instead, I manage to feel like part of a team.

He emerges half-bent over, muttering around the mug held to his mouth with both hands as if one wouldn't support it. "Wow! Strong!"

"I hate weak coffee." I was going to say "wimpy," but that seemed gratuitous. We have plenty of things to judge each other about; coffee doesn't need to be one of them. My brother takes another sip, makes a face, takes another. He settles himself onto one of Emily's plastic deck chairs, groaning on his way down. "You okay?"

"Oh, the lower back gives me trouble," as if the lower back didn't belong to him. "Especially early in the morning."

"You pretty much sit in one position all day, don't you?"

"I guess." He feels criticized. I don't think I was criticizing.

Emphasizing the warmth I honestly do feel, maybe overdoing it to the point of sounding fake, I say, "It must be kind of fun, talking to people from all over the country about their gardening questions." In point of fact it sounds deadly dull to me, but I'm hoping it's fun for him.

"It's just a job." Stepping over toys on the deck, he winces and presses a fist against his back.

"You're really in pain. Have you seen a doctor?"

"It's just middle-age aches and pains. You know."

"Oh, yeah. My massage therapist is practically part of my extended family."

"Well, we don't have a lot of massage therapists out here."

"I'm pretty good at it myself. I've paid attention to what she does to me." When he doesn't take the hint, I make the offer explicit. "Want a back rub? Martin has trouble with his shoulder and I can sometimes loosen it up for him."

I think he looks alarmed and embarrassed. "That's okay," he says, obviously meaning, "Hell, no."

"I get a massage every couple of weeks. I can always tell when it's time." My need to stretch is suddenly urgent, but for some reason I'm not comfortable doing that in front of him.

"We live different lives, Alexandra. Sorry. Sandi."

Now there's the start to any of a number of conversations. I pick one. "Are you happy with your life, Will? Have things turned out the way you hoped they would?" To my own ears I sound pleading, which makes me suspicious of my own motives: Do I want assurance that he's satisfied with his life because he's my brother and I love him, or because I need some sort of absolution from him for having left? Or am I hoping he'll confess to misery that will justify the path I've taken?

His shrug looks as if it hurts. I realize Daddy makes the same gesture. "I don't know. I don't think about it much."

"At least you have something you love. Not everybody can say that." I'm pushing too hard, but I can't seem to stop myself. I want to be assured that he's all right, whether he is or not. "At least you have your gardening."

"I hate gardening."

I stare at him, not really as surprised as I let on. "No, you don't." The absurdity of that makes me laugh, but I don't take it back. "You love gardening. You've always loved gardening, ever since we were kids. It's part of who you are."

"You're right, it's part of who I am. And I hate it. I hate the feel of dirt. I have to force myself to go out and pull weeds. Even moving the hoses is drudgery. Every year I pray for an early killing frost. And," here his voice actually breaks, "I've come to dread spring."

I'm not ready to concede. "But practically every time I hear from Emily she talks about your garden. She makes it sound as if that's just about all you do."

"It is just about all I do. At work I talk about gardening all day, I'm surrounded by gardening supplies and seed catalogues and greenhouses"—he shudders—"and people who consider it unnatural and immoral not to love gardening. And at home what do I do? I garden." On a roll now, he leans forward, grimacing, and very nearly shouts. "Plant! Fertilize! Water! Trim, weed, mulch! This year I doubled the size of the strawberry patch, even though the plants I already had bore only a few berries and the birds got those. Compost, transplant, separate bulbs! I take classes to learn how to do *more* gardening. In the winter I read gardening books. I subscribe to half a dozen gardening magazines. Carol and the kids give me gardening-related presents for every Christmas and birthday and Father's Day, and I don't blame them, it's my only interest."

"Why—"

"And I'm no good at it."

"Oh—"

"There is such a thing as a green thumb, and I don't have it."

"Oh, that can't be true—"

He's off on another litany now, this one of his horticultural failures and disappointments. The pervasiveness of the list (even *I* can grow petunias and zucchini) astonishes me, and his ferocity scares me a little, even in its comical extreme. I wait for him to finish. When he pauses, I have the impression he could go on for a lot longer, and hastily I interject. "Why do you do it then?"

He looks at me blankly. "Do what?"

The question confuses me. "Garden. Isn't that what we're talking about? Why do you garden if you hate it?"

"You said it yourself," he answers bitterly. "Gardening is part of who I am. It's how I make the world a better place."

The two of us recite together, "The Kove family *will* bring good into this world."

"Where's my mom and dad?" It's Erin, the gangly eleven-year-old, the worrier, wide-awake in a Pooh nightshirt. In the wash of sunlight, she looks a lot like her Uncle Will.

"They're at the hospital having your new brother or sister."

"It's a girl," she declares smugly. "Her name's Ebony."

"Whose idea was that?"

"Mine."

"Ebony?"

This strikes Will and me funny at the same instant, and we howl with laughter. Erin, of course, is insulted. I gasp, "I thought for sure it would be Eight," which causes a fresh onslaught of hilarity. Cutting her eyes at us and heaving a put-upon sigh, she retreats inside, and cartoon babble courses out through the door she didn't exactly slam.

This is not her room. It was her room for only a min-uscule fraction of its existence, and then not hers alone. The conceit that a space retains the personalities of its inhabitants is hogwash. There is no evidence, physical or otherwise, that it was once hers and Emily's; at the time, those few years, it would have been hard to imagine as anything else. When the children were at home—all of them; some of them; one or another of them temporarily returning—I thought I would never be done with raising them. In fact, child-rearing has occupied a small percentage of my life.

My mind wanders. I feel decidedly off-kilter, as if insufficiently rested. Then I remember: Alexandra and I were both awakened by Earl's pre-dawn phone call. I heard her answer, and later I read her note. Birth is the only good news likely to be delivered at that hour, and even then the adrenaline hurtling one out of sleep is unpleasant. Time being somewhat elastic for me these days, I had not realized the baby was to be born so soon. I do, in fact, feel a very mild interest.

Of greater interest, however, is my search of this room in which my daughter Alexandra has taken up very temporary residence. This little reconnaissance mission was unplanned, opportunistic. She is likely to be gone for some time. I will gather what information I can, and I have a perfect right to do so. She is a guest in my house.

On the dresser, angled to reflect in the mirror at the same time that it shows frontally to the room at large, is the portrait of my daughter and her family. Balancing it between my palms so as not to leave prints, I consider it in both shadow and light. I barely know these people. Her husband is black as a crow; the highlights on his cheekbones are blue. The boy must have some Indian in him, for the black hair is straight and the bridge of the nose squared. The girl is clearly a mulatto. Posed in the centre of the grouping, Alexandra is large, fair-skinned, beaming; her husband's hands are on her shoulders and she has an arm around each of the youngsters, as if they were related to her.

For long moments I study the photo, waiting in vain for some internal response I might term familial. These people are alien. They are not my kind. They are not her kind, either, and I am furious with her for putting me in the position of reacting this way.

When I set the picture back on the dresser, the flimsy cardboard brace collapses and it tips over face-first with a tiny sharp slap. I force myself to stand it upright, but cannot quite get the proper angle. An image floods my mind, fully formed and with every sense engaged, of the instant Alexandra sees it has been moved, then the instant she realizes I must be the mover, the intruder.

The headache that has been with me off and on all my life ratchets up a notch or two, and I must sit down. Groping, I find the bed, unmade, and as my fists take some of my weight my knees buckle, so that I collapse face down among the sheets and blankets. I lie still, waiting for things to right themselves, dimly wondering, and not for the first time, whether I will have the wherewithal to end all this when the time comes, whether I will even know when the time has come.

Eli and Evan have been up less than fifteen minutes when they are embroiled in one of those utterly irresolvable squabbles, this one apparently over Cheerios, reminding me how similar fourteen- and five-year-olds can be. Erin's haughty comments to and about them are intended both to demonstrate her moral superiority (what eleven-year-old girls self-righteously call "being mature") and to rile them further. Helpful Will is making noises about having to get to work.

"I thought we'd hear from Earl by now," I fret aloud to him as he drains his second cup of coffee, apparently having gotten used to the way I make it.

"It takes longer than this to have a baby. You remember—oh, no, you don't, do you?"

On the working assumption that this is said benevolently, I grin. "See? Adoption's easier."

By the way he looks at me I know what he's going to say. Serves me right for opening the subject. "So, what? You couldn't have kids of your own?"

"Our children *are* our own."

"You know what I mean. Okay, okay, you're right. I'm sorry. I take your point."

Somewhat mollified, I say with less vitriol than I might have otherwise, "That's an awfully personal question, don't you think?"

He shrugs and gets to his feet. "Hey, sis, we're family. We're *supposed* to be in each other's business."

There's actually something kind of sweet and disarming about this. "We chose to adopt," I inform him, my tone distressingly like Erin's. "Neither of us has any reason to believe we couldn't have birth children."

He shakes his head. "I don't get it."

This "you must be crazy," along with Emily's "you're heroes," are the two most common reactions when people learn about our kids. I never know what to say. Now I hear myself asking him, "What does Daddy say about it?"

"Nothing."

"Nothing?" I sound, and feel, forlorn. Then I see that he's lying, or withholding. "Will?"

" 'Alexandra always has to do everything *differently*.' " He spits the last word. " 'She does it to get back at me.' "

"That's what he says?"

"That's what he said. I think I only heard him say anything about it that one time."

"But he's the one who taught us to think for ourselves and do things our own way. You know, the goddamn road less travelled by."

"Dad? You've got to be kidding. He controls every move we make. Always has, always will. Why do you think I'm a gardener?"

"He told you to be a gardener? Come on, Will."

"What he's told me over and over, from as far back as I can remember, is that flowers and home-grown vegetables are good for us and good for the world and he always wanted to grow them himself but couldn't. So he gave it to me. I'm designated to do it for him. His surrogate gardener."

"But you said you're not good at it."

"I'm not. By far more stuff dies than grows, and I have puny little harvests."

"So why'd he choose you?"

"He made a mistake, I guess." He laughs humourlessly. "I guess he taught me wrong."

"How do you think he gave it to you, Will? I mean, he gave me stuff like that, too, sort of assignments, and it's always felt like more than just teaching. Almost as if—I don't know, as if he actually put something into me."

Will is quiet for a long time. I don't know what that means.

After a while I sit up. The headache has receded, a familiar lying in wait until its services are required again. As often happens in these interludes between pain and nausea, my thought processes seem clear, although the possibility always exists that this is a delusion. I stand up, brace myself against the wall until I can trust my balance, and walk across the room.

The manuscript of her novel, insolently titled Fatherland, is still in the drawer. I remove the first chapter, twenty-one pages, and sit in the desk chair to read. I cannot determine whether she has worked on it, even touched it, even thought about it since she has been in my house. I stare down at it for long moments, and then slide the box out of the drawer and sit on the bed with it heavy on my lap. Then I take off the lid.

Finally I can't stand it anymore, and I change the direction if not the content of the conversation. "So you've spent your life doing something you don't want to do so he could have fresh tomatoes?"

It's a stupid thing to say, and he's right to narrow his eyes at me. "Something like that," he says to close down the conversation, which is fine with me. From inside the house Erin screams bloody murder. "I've got to get to work," Will says brightly, his hand already on the gate. "It's all yours, Aunt Sandi."

Sighing, I get to my feet and enter the fray.

It is good. It is shockingly good. I am taking a terrible risk. I read chapter one straight through, finding very little to object to, and then read it again.

Eli calls Erin an asshole. Erin yells triumphantly, "I'm telling!" Evan is chanting at the top of his voice; I don't understand the words, but the tone is clearly smart-ass. The phone rings.

Chapter 7

"Hi, Daddy."

"Good afternoon." He gives a pale, grey nod. He's mad at me. I have no idea why, and after spending the day at Emily's I'm too tired and worried to play games with this selfish old man who withholds everything from everybody and then has the balls to act like the aggrieved party.

Apparently I'm now the designated bad-news-bearer, on top of all the other familial designations I've re-acquired since I've been back. Obediently, I announce, "I have bad news."

"About the infant."

I bite back the "fuck you" that springs to my lips, settling for infusing "the infant's" name with as much vitriol as I can. "Bella. About Bella, yes." He says nothing. He just sits there. "The doctors are saying she was born with cerebral atrophy. She has only about a third of her brain."

Silence. He gives no indication he's heard or comprehended what I said, or that it's of any interest to him whatsoever.

Pity and disgust sicken me, as well as fury that my daughter Emily has failed her child-bearing responsibility—all I have ever expected of her. If her sister is correct, what she has borne can be considered human only in the most technical sense. I refute and refuse any relation to it.

"Probably she won't live more than a few weeks, but they say there are cases where kids like this live five or ten years."

This has nothing to do with me. This cannot have anything to do with me.

When the old bastard just sits there stony-faced saying nothing, I figure I've done my part and duck past him to use the phone. It's still on the triangular knickknack shelf in the most public corner of the kitchen, which used to make me crazy when I was a teenager. I'd use my cell phone if I could get decent reception in these damned woods.

Tara answers, knows to accept the charges. "Hi, honey."

"Hi, Mommy. What's wrong?"

"What makes you think something's wrong?"

"You sound funny."

"I'm—tired. And I miss you guys."

"Are you mad at me?"

From the first, Tara has been exquisitely attuned to my moods, accurately perceiving when something's bothering me but unable to distinguish fatigue from anger from work-related stress from preoccupation with something I'm writing from worry over her or her brother. Unlike Ramon, who usually just figures I'm being a bitch for some reason having nothing to do with him, Tara takes the default position that I'm mad at her, I've stopped loving her, I'm going to abandon her in one way or another like every other mother she's known. At least now she can ask, and more or less believe my answer, instead of cutting herself or smearing feces. I kick myself now for having dissembled with her; being away from her for so long is already skating on pretty thin abandonment ice.

So I tell her at least part of the truth, which is sometimes the best we can do. "Your Aunt Emily is having a hard time."

"Because of the baby? Bella?"

"Yes."

"That's a really weird name."

"I think it's a lovely name."

"But it doesn't start with E."

"You're right."

"Is Bella, like, sick?"

I say. "Not sick, exactly, but she was born with only part of her brain."

"Eeew. Gross. Why? How does that happen? Did Aunt Emily do something wrong?"

"The doctors don't know why. Sometimes things like that just happen."

"Is she going to die?"

I don't tell her we're all going to die. She knows that, better than most children her age, and it's not what she means. "She probably won't live very long."

"When are you coming home?"

"I'll be there when you get back from soccer camp, okay?" It isn't okay with her, or with me, either; I don't know why adults say that to kids, as if we're asking for their complicity, when what we really mean is, "Okay? Do you understand?" Of course they don't.

"I miss you," she says with heartbreaking simplicity.

"I miss you, too. Are you being nice to Daddy?"

"I guess."

"You'll have a good time at camp. You always do."

"I guess."

"How's Ramon?"

"Fine. He's a brat."

"Can I talk to him?"

"He's at his girlfriend's," she sneers.

Keenly disappointed, even a little jealous, I make a point of identifying for her the tension she'll pick up in my voice. "Oh, I was hoping to talk to him. I miss him, too."

"Why do you miss *Ramon*?"

She knows why. She likes to hear me say it. I oblige; I like saying it, too. "Because he's my son and I love him."

"Oh."

"Is Daddy there?"

"He went to the store."

At thirteen, she ought to be plenty old enough to stay by herself, of course, but I'm not confident that she is. "Are you okay staying home alone?"

"Mom. I'm not a baby."

I swallow hard. "Will you have Dad call me at Grandpa's when he gets back?" Grandpa. Aunt Emily. These relational terms must mean next to nothing to her, since she's never met these people. Or maybe, given Tara's devotion to family and evident understanding of the many nuances of the word, she already knows better than I do what it means to be related to my sister, her aunt, and my father, her grandfather, and the new baby Bella, her cousin, my niece.

She says she'll give her dad the message. I tell her to write it down, and can practically see her rolling her eyes as she informs me she already did. We say "I love you" to each other, and I hang up feeling utterly bereft.

My father calls, "Alexandra! Come here!" the minute I hang up, and whether I obey him or not I'm still the child to his parent. I go and stand in the doorway but assert my independence by not sitting down. He fixes me with his trademark hawk-like stare but doesn't say anything, so I don't say anything, either, and I meet and hold his gaze. There's a long, taut, stubborn silence.

She is lying. She is withholding information. I will not have this. "What," I finally demand, "is going on?"

"What do you mean?"

She knows perfectly well what I mean. "What is wrong with your sister?"

When we were kids, "don't tell Daddy" was our mantra, and telling Daddy the surest way to get back at a sibling even if he didn't mete out a punishment. So I feel both guilty and smug when I tell him, "Postpartum depression." He snorts, as if to let me know he knows I'm making this up. I defend myself by going into detail.

"She's not eating or sleeping much. She can't take care of herself, let alone the kids. She doesn't have any milk to nurse the baby."

Alexandra says these outrageous and unacceptable things to me as if she is making a PowerPoint presentation at a corporate conference. She is calm and collected, voice well-modulated, body relaxed and alert. Her self-possession appals me, although I gave it to her.

127

Who is this? What is she doing in my house? She is an intruder of the worst sort. What has she done with my daughter?

He just stares at me. I swear he doesn't blink, like a goddamn snake. He expects me to do something. I have no idea what or how. He just stares at me. Finally I leave the room.

In a gesture of blatant disrespect, she leaves the room. If she leaves the house I am not aware of it, yet I do not hear her anywhere in it. Into my mind surge thoughts and images of the defective infant, with the insinuation that she is in some way related to me, and I banish them.

What I want to do is leave the old bastard once and for all, leave this dumpy little house in this claustrophobic little woods once and for all and go home. What I do is retreat into the room I've been assigned. I need to sit and think about Bella, until at least the shock subsides if not the sorrow and horror and all the rest of it. I need to come to terms with Emily's despair in order to calm my instinct to stay away. I need to write, though not yet about babies born with incomplete brains, not yet about Bella herself. Maybe, though, about despair.

The minute I shut the door behind me I know he's been in here. I'd be hard pressed to say how I know.

More than a feeling, not exactly a smell or a taste, nothing visual or auditory about it, the sense that tells me of my father's intrusion is highly specialized and reliable.

This is his house; he has a right to be anywhere in it he chooses. But my movements become self-consciously gingerly, stealthy, so as not to contaminate the crime scene.

The family portrait on the dresser has been moved; I put it back in the right place. The desk drawer isn't completely closed. The lid of the manuscript box is askew, and I force myself to ease it all the way off. His tiny, blunt-pencilled handwriting dirties the title page, cluttering up the white space around the title *Fatherland*. His comment on the title itself is: "Obvious. Too broad."

It's been a long time now since I got one of those small white envelopes with my name—"A. Kove"—in the centre and his name—"A. Kove"—in the upper left-hand corner, one or two or ten sheets of pocket-sized notebook paper fringed along one side or across the top where they'd been torn from the spiral. Reading his dense script required a conscious shift from left to right brain, as if listening to experimental jazz or looking at an abstract painting.

This is the same edgy thrill I felt back then, certain every time that a secret vital to my life would now be revealed. It never was. The letters never told me anything new, and I haven't kept any of them. When I mentioned to Emily that Daddy sometimes wrote to me, she snapped that it wasn't fair for the one who'd left to get all the attention, as if running away had made me better than the rest of them.

Now my father has had the balls not only to read my manuscript but also to edit it. Flipping through the 312 pages, I see with growing incredulity that he's made notations on nearly every one. At first glance some appear to be just grammar and punctuation corrections, which really pisses me off. Not a few, though, are paragraphs, skinny in a side margin or filling up the top or bottom white space, occasionally—as indicated by a stern dark arrow—extending over onto the back of a page.

Nobody's holding a gun to my head. I don't have to read what he's written. He can try to give me shit but I don't have to take it.

I pace. I brace myself against the dresser and the doorjamb. I sit down and stand up and sit down again, repositioning the desk chair several times in an attempt to get good reading light through the window. I prop my feet on the bed, but that's too high so I rearrange myself again with my feet on my briefcase. I put the box with the whole manuscript in my lap, intending to take out a page at a time, but that's awkward. After experimenting with several other systems, I finally settle for leaving the box on the floor and working with a chapter at a time. I try three or four pens before one suits me. Then, finally, I set to work deciphering my father's unsolicited comments on what feels like—though it manifestly is not—my life's work.

Time seems to pass. Ambient light becomes more grey than yellow. Chill enters the house, which confuses me regarding the time of day and season of the year, and I drift outside, where rain is dripping through grey-yellow leaves and underfoot are layers of unavoidable things I will do my best to avoid by sending my daughter Alexandra where I myself cannot possibly go. If I can find her. I must find her.

By the time I reach about page thirteen, I've realized I can't read a lot of his writing, but I don't let myself believe it until the end of Part I on page sixty-six. Even then I randomly sample through the rest of the book before I give up.

I can make out letters—o's and e's and a's closed so firmly they're almost solid, t's with perfectly horizontal crosses and i's dotted precisely above their points. A few individual words and phrases are legible—"good" on page twenty-three, "trite" on pages 132 and 246, "nonsense" on page eleven, "derivative of Dickinson" on page 301 (perilously near the end)—but the surrounding comments are indecipherable so I don't know *what* he thought was good, trite, nonsense, derivative, or why. Most frustrating, entire paragraphs and pages of his carefully reasoned and closely formed critique are utterly unreadable.

The temptation is strong to crumple the pages and throw them across the room. Better yet, to dump the whole fucking box in the trash or burn it in the fireplace or, melodramatically, bury it in the woods. When I get home it would be easy enough to print out a clean copy, all my words still there and none of his.

Instead, I get to my feet, heft the manuscript box in both hands, and stride out of the room. Enough already. The son-of-a-bitch is going to tell me what he means and what he knows.

He's gone.

Of course he's gone. I'm ready to have it out with him, if not once and for all, at least for once. So what possessed me to think he'd be sitting there waiting for me? He won't make it easy. Well, neither will I.

He's not in his chair or anywhere else in the living room. He's not in the kitchen or the mud room. I look behind the open bathroom door and the shower curtain to make sure he hasn't collapsed in there. I knock on his bedroom door, call through it, finally open it and go in far enough to see that he's not there. He's not in what passes for the yard. Cursory phone calls to the homes of my siblings confirm he isn't with any of them, except for Vaughn who, naturally, doesn't answer his phone.

I start out of the house with the manuscript still in my hands, think better of it, return it at first hastily and then carefully to its drawer. Empty-handed, I leave to track my father down.

He can't have gone far. He's eighty-one years old—yeah, yeah, Galen, eighty-two. He's somewhere in these yellow woods, and I will fucking find him.

I am walking through the wood. I suppose this is the wood. I suppose this is walking. Two roads, at the very least, diverge here. The phrase about two roads in a yellow wood is familiar. A line of poetry, I believe. Perhaps one I composed in a spurt of creativity so long past it scarcely seems my own. No, of course, it is from a poem by Robert Frost, one of my long-time favourites.

Searching, the free-fall sensation of searching without an object.

Searching. For someone—my daughter—my daughter Alexandra. I have not seen her for a lifetime or more. Would I know her if I found her?

Searching for an infant, a baby girl, come into this world and this family deformed. Like so much else, asking too much of me. No relation to me in any real sense. Not really even of the same species, for much of what defines "human" is lacking. She is something other, something alien. Or I am.

Alexandra. I have the impression that it is someone named Alexandra I am hunting for, and then that it is not.

Hunting. Have I already hunted for her here? Hunted her? In this little glade? Under this tree? In this den, behind this rock, inside that yellow house? Searching.

Searching is futile. Searching is always futile. Futility leads me to a cave under a rock ledge where I may or may not have been before. A snake loops around the entrance. I have the foolish impression that the snake has a name and a relationship to me, but then it is gone, both the snake and the impression are gone, and good riddance. I know to drop to hands and knees, though the motion causes vertigo and my hands and knees ache from impact with the spongy ground. Almost prostrate to crawl inside, I am out of breath and aching. I seem to be both lost and at home.

Suddenly all is clear. I must find my daughter Alexandra, or cause her to find me, in order to give her the next assignment. She is to love the infant, the infant Bella, because I dare not, and because my life is over.

It's the hideout I need to find first, for what seems like the umpteenth time, but I still don't know where it is. I swear there are no landmarks; everything I notice looks like every other tree, dead tree, snake, pile of brush, chipmunk (or are those woodchucks?), bird, rock.

Hardly ten minutes have passed before I'm in a panic, convinced this is the day, this is the moment he intends to kill himself, out of despondency or rage over Bella or a weird sort of competition with her. Stealing the suicide recipe now seems a flimsy stratagem. Why didn't I tell somebody? I know perfectly well why and it disgusts me—it was our secret, Daddy's and mine, and I didn't want to share it with anybody.

Now I can only hope he won't be able to find the cave, or won't remember what the bottles and bags are for. But it's just as likely he'll be in one of his phases of acute clarity. Where is senile dementia when you need it?

Where is she? What will I do without her? I have been here before. She has left me before. She has left me again. I will not do this again. I will not go back. A thousand paths diverge. I am lost. I huddle in this dim, small space, full of snakes.

I scream and jump back when something slithers right across my shoe. This pisses me off. I am not afraid of snakes. When we were growing up, Daddy wouldn't have put up with it, and I've always prided myself on not being girly about this sort of thing. It's just that I didn't see it coming. I'm not scared, just startled. I kick savagely at the mounded leaf duff, but naturally the stupid little serpent has wrinkled and is long gone.

Emily won't hold her baby, won't touch her, won't look at her. Earl and the other kids are keeping Bella alive, though she won't live long no matter what they do. Emily spends her time in bed or, at most, sitting up in a chair in the dim bedroom. She speaks very little, eats less, may not be sleeping at all.

I hold Bella every chance I get. I can't get enough of her.

A baby shares this place with me. She changes shape as I look at her, tear my gaze away, helplessly look back. Wide eyes with no light in them, or, more precisely, with an unnatural light. Mouth working. Pale strangled cry. Skull like clay that does not harden, ready at any given moment to ooze between my fingers.

Out of the gloom around me dozens of containers emerge, bottles and bags and boxes, and in each of them floats the disembodied head of this one baby girl. She wants something of me, and plainly she is entitled, but I have nothing to spare.

For me this loamy scent is primal, because I haven't lived for a very long time in a place damp enough to be loamy. It scares me that I don't wish Martin were here.

There's a rock overhang, but it gives no external sign of creating and then sheltering an inhabitable space. I tiptoe closer, crouch, peer, and see him at once, hear him lightly breathing.

Though we're facing each other head-on and not three feet apart, he doesn't acknowledge me. Knees drawn up and elbows splayed, he looks like a praying mantis, and I'm surprised he can still sit like that at his age—I'm not sure I could. He may in fact be praying, which doesn't seem as out of character as I'd have thought; his hands are clasped at his chest.

Then he raises his hands and tilts back his head, and light from somewhere glints on the bottle from which he's about to drink. I lunge at him, falling short and scraping my shoulder and howling, "Daddy! No! Not yet!"

Chapter 8

Alexandra's interference takes me entirely by surprise—as though further evidence were required that I am failing, in every sense of the word. I should have seen it coming. Not so long ago, I would have.

Trance shattered, pulse shot wild and thin, body and soul set to quivering, I nevertheless manage not to drop the flask or spill its contents. For all the time and effort spent on this concoction, all the retrieving and decoding of notes, all the gathering and scavenging, all the planting and tending and harvesting, all the meticulous measuring and re-measuring, I cannot be sure I have done everything correctly, or, even if so, that it will have the intended effect. Still, I would not like to waste it.

In a caricature of what in contemporary American parlance is called an enabler, she wrests the flask away from me and empties it between us. The ground, always nearly saturated here, refuses to accept this additional moisture, causing a small pool to form. We will both get our feet wet and catch our death.

"How dare you?" I mean to shout, but my voice is reedy and I must pause for breath after just those three syllables. When I can, I add, "Who do you think you are?"

"Who do you think you are?" Among my least favourite of his many catchphrases—right up there with "Alexandra, pay attention," and "Alexandra, slow down," and "the Kove family *will* bring good into this world"—it especially infuriates me here and now.

"I'm your daughter! I'm your daughter, goddammit, and you can't do this to me! Not yet!" Not yet? What am I saying?

"Emily?"

"Don't give me that bullshit. You know perfectly well who I am. Sandi. Your daughter Sandi."

"I have no daughter named Sandi."

"Alexandra, all right? Your daughter Alexandra."

"My daughter Alexandra has been gone for many years."

"Stop it, Daddy! You know who I am!"

Now I do know who she is, but what has become the pretence of confusion may be useful a while longer. With rather more aversion than I actually feel, I recoil from her touch, and am gratified and stricken by the look on her face.

139

*From somewhere there is music, a romantic would
say from the wood itself. But if there is such a thing
as music of the spheres, if the earth can be said to sing
and this yellow wood among all others to harmonize, it
is only because of the limitations of human language
and perception. This is Vaughn, no more or less. It must
be Vaughn, although in my experience he has not made
quite this sort of music. I believe it is a harp. The image
of burly, dishevelled Vaughn lugging a harp through the
wood strikes me as comical.*

"Don't laugh at me!"

He stops laughing but his whole body signifies
contemptuous amusement as he manages in the
cramped space of the cave—I can't believe I'm in a
cave—to turn his back on me. I swear there's harp
music close by. Could my crazy brother be playing
a harp out here in the middle of nowhere? Does
Daddy have a radio or a tape or CD player in here,
maybe to create an atmosphere appropriate for
killing himself or whatever other magic he likes
to think he's working? I swear Herpie or some
less familiar snake is dangling from the ceiling,
but then the serpentine shadow melds with the
general gloom.

These people are nuts. This is where I come from,
and these people are fucking insane.

"Oh, God," she says contemptuously, "don't tell me you wrote a suicide note."

I did, and folded it into a plain white envelope, and propped it against the small cairn of roundish rocks I built for this purpose just inside the entrance. Then I more or less forgot about it. Now that she mentions it, I think how inappropriate it would be for anyone to read this missive, since as it happens I am not going to die by my own hand to̲___ She h___ ___f_l___e for the paper; I reach it before s___ ___ my jacket. Like the elixir she has ___ he letter may be of use to me at s___ ___ut only if there have been no pr___ ___.

"What a selfis___ ___ the temerity to say to me. As if l___ ___; as if, precisely because I am he___ ___to say to me on the subject.

Never in my life have I been selfish. Always, and to a fault, I have looked for opportunities to put others—the whole world of others—before my self. And before my children—had I been selfish, I would have put my own children first. Never having had children of her own, Alexandra would not understand this concept.

"How the hell do you think everybody would feel if you killed yourself?" I did not teach her this indelicate manner of speaking. "How do you think I would feel?"

"Relieved" comes to mind, and "purposeless," but saying either would lead into a discussion both distracting and *pointless. In order to protect both myself and her, I say nothing.*

She takes me by the shoulders. My daughter, this large woman, actually takes me by the shoulders. Her grasp causes pain in my shoulders, neck, back, hips. "You're holding something back from me," she snarls. "Something that's mine. I'm not leaving," she whispers, and shakes me, and leans close enough that I can hear her words, smell her coffee breath, see the creases of middle age at the corners of her mouth. "You hear me? I'm not leaving until you give me what's mine. And neither are you."

I will not accede. I will pass along to her what I choose, at the time and in the form I choose. I am the parent, she the child; I am the sorcerer, she the apprentice. Neither of us has dared to forget what we are to each other.

As a diversionary tactic, with enough truth in it to make it plausible, I say, "I want you to love Bella for both of us." The infant's name, my granddaughter's name, burns my tongue.

Stunned, I stare at him—not quite at his eyes, which make no pretence of meeting mine. His face is so frightful, and I realize with yet another shock wave, so dear to me that I don't think I've ever before had the courage to look at it straight on. My father's face is small. I could hold it in my hands. Grabbing him is wildly disrespectful and wildly intimate at the same time, intimacy with my father being by definition disrespectful. This contact with his thin flesh and brittle bone is too much for me, and I take my hands away. We both sit back. His face is in deep shadow now. With much more courage than it ought to take simply to talk to one's father, I demand, "Just how does that work, Daddy? I've always wondered. Vaughn's music and Will's gardening and Emily's kids and Galen's causes and all the things you cursed and blessed me with—keeping in touch with your friends and family when you can't be bothered, accepting and loving all kinds of people you can't tolerate anywhere near you, writing, something now having to do with Bella—how do you put all that shit on us? Or in us, or whatever? And why does it absolve you to make us do what you can't do?"

He scoots around, an undignified motion that embarrasses me. His gaze is a searchlight, first on me but then swinging past to the cave opening. He scoots toward it on his butt; I can hardly stand to watch. I'm sure he's going to bump his head, but he doesn't.

"I do not know why." He tosses the words back like crumbs over his shoulder, more hunched than ever as he manoeuvres himself out of the cave. It's an answer to only the second part of my question, and not really even that. I wish to hell he'd use contractions. "But it is the most I have ever been able to do. And it is something."

His feet are out of the cave now; I don't want to be imagining them sticking out like narrow little animals. Now his thin shanks—I can't imagine anybody but my father having body parts called "shanks"—and knobby knees. Now his torso is silhouetted against the yellow-green light outside the cave. Now he's out. With difficulty, he gets to his feet and hobbles off.

Why does he presume I won't just stay here and poke through his goddamn wizard's lair? Maybe he knows I already have. More likely he thinks I don't have the *chutzpah.* Or he has no more secrets worth finding. Or he's smugly feathered this nest with them precisely for me to find and marvel at.

It's not easy for somebody my size to crawl, but I crawl out, stand, get my bearings, start off in the direction I think he's gone. A movement ahead turns out to be a branch in a slight breeze. A movement underfoot turns out to be the snake to whom I find myself muttering, "Make yourself useful, why don't you? Where's Daddy?" I don't expect a reply, and I don't get one.

This gets old fast. I think I'll just go back to Bella's house and hold that baby girl some more while I can.

I let myself in Earl and Emily's creaky back gate. A family congregation is on deck in my direct line of sight the minute I'm inside the yard. Not at all sure I'm welcome to join it, I almost retreat into the woods again. Gathered in the slanted afternoon shade are Earl and Emily and some or all of their children. Compulsively I make a mental list: Eddie, Elizabeth, Eve, Eileen, Eli, Erin, Evan. All their children but one. Where is Bella?

Emily has her back to me and is surrounded by her family, but I can hear her crying. Many of the others are crying, too. Earl's arms twine around as many of his family as he can reach. He can't seem to reach Bella.

There's Vaughn, coming around the side of the house or maybe through it—from this vantage point I can't tell what path he's taken or blazed to get here. In greenish pants and a tan hooded sweat-shirt, hair tangled like leaves, he brings to mind a wood sprite even though he's big and bearded and not particularly light on his feet—except, I guess, in the mocking sense of the phrase my father's generation would have used. Even more musical tools than usual increase his bulk, his clumsiness, and his noise level—single bells, rows of bells on straps, bells at his belt and cuffs and around the edge of his hood; castanets on fingertips and snare drums at waist and a cymbal under one arm; under the other arm a trumpet and some kind of long looping horn; a harmonica on an awkward frame around his neck; flutes and tiny dulcimers and other things to be blown into and plucked sticking like arrows out of the open pack on his back.

And he's lugging a full-size harp. He lumbers up the three steps to the deck and sets the harp down. It rocks slightly, strings and graceful frame patterning the yellow light, then settles into place. I move forward. Earl sees me and beckons with a gesture of his head. I move closer but not quite into the group.

Vaughn turns to Emily and hesitates, then holds out his arms. Her weeping rises into a wail. Others join, even me. Emily goes to Vaughn and he gently takes from her a bundle I now see she is holding. I know, of course, what it is.

For a long moment Vaughn holds the bundle awkwardly, tenderly, in the crook of his arm along with the horns, and then with heartbreaking care lays it at the base of the harp. He kneels, his attitude reverent. My skin prickles. Very carefully he unwraps the pale yellow blanket.

I knew it was Bella, but I was not prepared for her. For how silent she is. For how perfect she looks, dappled and at this little distance. For the way my brother exposes her to both her parents' protected yard and the wild yellow woods. Most fiercely I'm ambushed by my instant conviction that she is dead, and then by the slight movement, slight noise that tells me she is not.

Quiet lamentation makes a canopy over all of us. Vaughn sits on a deck chair, which is not quite the right height, and rests his big hands one on each side of the web of harp strings. Then his fingers begin to move, and I close my eyes and hold my breath for the exquisite sorrow of the music. There is a while when the human sound of mourning obscures the sound of the harp. But then the music plunges and soars and takes us all with it.

I don't see Daddy anywhere. I don't know what I'm supposed to do. I find myself creeping forward. I'll think later about why I don't just leave and why I don't just walk upright to join the group. I stand slightly outside, until Earl, of all people, takes my hand and pulls me in.

The baby is naked in the warm shade. Her eyes are open, but utterly unfocused. The music ripples around her, around all of us. Emily sinks to the slatted surface of the deck, several arm lengths from her daughter. Bella's open mouth is a tiny hole; misshapen by both present circumstance and the circumstances of her own little life, it looks both perfect and hideously deformed. Her walnut-sized fists open and close like any other infant's, but much more rapidly, like trapped insects.

Abruptly, I need to feel her heartbeat. I have to touch her. Whether she knows the difference or not, I can't let either of us be alone while she dies. For I know that's what we're doing here; we're attending her death, with Vaughn the unlikely midwife-in-reverse.

I've fallen to my knees, too, and now I crawl between two of my nieces to the side of my niece who is leaving, at this very moment, in this very dappled place, in this company that can go with her only so far. Nobody stops me. Vaughn's harp makes a web around us, drawing us together but not too tightly, not impermeably. Bella doesn't know me, doesn't care that I'm here.

Lying beside her on the deck, I gather her to me. Nobody stops me. The keening soars. Someone's voice has gone into singing, sorrowful and lovely. I cradle the baby to my chest and lay my face against her soft, baby-smelling, distorted skull, aware of the open fontanel that now will never close, aware of her heartbeat and my own. The exquisite passion of Vaughn's music is almost unbearable, almost enough.

"Alexandra," my father says.

"Alexandra," I say, apparently aloud. "Alexandra, take her."

The damnable harp music stops, and Vaughn is looking at me like a man dispossessed. The funereal keening breaks up into disjointed curses and sobs. Earl advances on me. One of my sons, Will or Galen, puts a heavy hand on my shoulder, causing instant pain. Alexandra struggles to her feet with the baby precariously in her arms and says something to her sister, the mother of the child. I am escorted out of the yard and through the wood to my own house, where my son, Galen or Will, insists I sit down in my chair and stay there, himself sits on the couch to guard me. I have no objection. I have done all I can do.

Chapter 9

"It's August, Sandi. You've been gone six weeks."

"And three days. I could tell you how many hours." Literally sick with homesickness, nauseous, head pounding, chest burning, I make sure to tell him, "I miss you. I miss the kids. I want to come home." Swaddled against my chest, the baby Bella is silent, except for a whimpery breathing. Almost absently, I stroke her imperfectly shaped head.

"So come on home then." In his rich accent, it sounds like a song.

"I can't, Martin. There's no way Emily can take care of this baby. She's pretty much lost it. She hardly eats or sleeps. She can't take care of the kids—a lot of the time she doesn't seem to notice she has any. Earl tried to get the doctor to hospitalize her but they said she doesn't qualify. Fucking insurance."

Another husband might object that Emily has Earl and several grown or nearly grown children and a local extended family to take care of her and Bella, and that there's little reason to think my sticking around will be of help to her anyway. Another husband might remind me that he and our children need me at home, that I promised I'd be there when Tara got back from soccer camp and have reneged, that I've missed practically the entire summer with them. Might point out that nobody knows how long Bella will live, another day or another ten years, and surely I don't plan to stay here indefinitely, or to bring her home with me, and anyway what do I know about taking care of an infant with such extreme needs? Would, ultimately, be quite within his rights and the logic of the situation to insist it's crazy and presumptuous to think I have any responsibility in this matter. Hubris, really. Arrogant and dangerous.

Says Martin, *my* husband, "What a good sister you are." Another husband might intend sarcasm. His mild and pure sincerity unleashes my tears.

"I don't know about that." I can hardly talk. "Right now I don't feel much like a good sister. Or wife or mother or daughter." Or aunt. Especially aunt. But I don't say that. Why don't I say that to Martin, from whom I have no secrets? Is there something secret, then, about my relationship with this little girl?

"Ah, sweetheart."

"I think I'm staying as much for me as for Emily." I don't even really know what that means, and it's probably not a kind or fair thing to admit to the husband and children I've more or less abandoned, but now that I've said it, it feels true. Bella moves against me and I wonder whether in any sense she knows I'm here, and whether it matters.

"I do not understand." When Martin stops using contractions and his voice takes on that brittleness under its tropical lilt I know he's hurt. Or about to be.

I don't understand, either, and the thought of trying is exhausting, but I have to offer something to this loving and beloved man. Tucking the receiver against my shoulder, careful not to put pressure on any part of Bella's flaccid little body, I hug myself in an attempt to stop the trembling. Bella makes a small noise. "There are secrets here, Martin. Secrets I have to know. Something having to do with Emily and Galen and Will and Vaughn and me, and the baby, and Daddy."

"Family secrets," he acknowledges. "Family legends."

Martin's family secrets are long ago, far away, and far-reaching. Well before we met he'd unearthed all that needed unearthing, so I heard about them in the past tense, already made into legends colourful and settled, if in some instances horrific, whose meanings were no longer open for interpretation or debate.

With what looks now like unbelievable naiveté, I'd thought mine were settled, too: "I come from a crazy family," and, "My mother left us when we were small and we never heard from her again," and, "My father's a control freak," had seemed all there was to it, with the handy summation, "I've learned to keep my distance."

In the beginning, when the subject of parents and siblings came up, Martin would assume a silence that I knew was inviting, or he'd prod a little, but I never had much to offer. I began to claim that his family in the Congo and his cousin in New York were my family, and in important ways they are.

For the adoption social workers I trotted out happy and sad and telling anecdotes from my childhood, all of them true, and described my sporadic and cursory contact with my family of origin in terms that made it sound regular. I didn't mention my mother's abandonment or my father's powers; there was no way they could know anything about my past if I didn't tell them, and these things were just too complicated—not painful or distressing or important, mind you—to get into.

When Ramon, and more often Tara, have asked about their aunts and uncles and cousins and grandparents on my side, I've had a few standard responses. "Your Grandpa Alex is a strange man. We're not very close. You have three uncles and an aunt and a whole slew of cousins. Maybe you'll meet them someday. I don't know when. Maybe someday." What's happening now, to my intense surprise and discomfort, is that a legend is taking shape on the spot, with me in it.

"Why must you know?" Martin inquires, perfectly reasonably. "Why can secrets not remain secrets?"

Taken aback, all I can come up with is, "I feel as if I'm on the brink of something," which isn't an answer.

"A precipice, perhaps?" He chuckles, one of the most beautiful sounds in the world.

I laugh, too, but it hurts. "Will you catch me if I fall off? Or pick up the pieces?"

"You betcha."

That makes me laugh again, less painfully this time. Bella stirs. "I don't know what's going on here, Martin. I don't know what I feel so goddamn compelled to find out."

"That's why you will stay a while."

"I'm sorry."

"No need for sorry. We're fine."

"Really?" Part of me doesn't want them to be doing "fine" without me.

Martin, bless his heart, knows exactly what to say. "We miss you. We all miss you. Things aren't the same around here without you. But we're okay."

Mollified, I move the conversation along. "I heard you took Tara and her friends for a hike in the mountains. You are a brave man."

"I had to pull over to the side of the road only twice to persuade them to control themselves in the car.

Perhaps it was the absence of guardrails that finally caught their attention."

"Tara said you saw bighorn sheep."

"I wouldn't have thought she noticed."

"I haven't talked to Ramon since I've been gone."

"I haven't talked to him much myself. He most definitely has his own life."

"I guess that's what we did this for, isn't it? If you do a good job as a parent, they leave you. How fucking fair is that?"

We laugh ruefully. It's only after we hang up—exchanging "I love you's," arranging a time for tomorrow's conversation, bemoaning our astronomical phone bills but not letting that stop us—that my own observation, that being a parent by definition means you'll be abandoned, makes me think of Daddy. And of Mom, who took the initiative and abandoned us first. I seem to be thinking of her a lot these days. I don't want to. She doesn't deserve to have any of us thinking about her.

I'm supposed to have Bella at Emily's in six minutes. I'm going to be late. Not that Emily will notice or care. I change Bella's diaper, though it's hardly damp, and bundle her into the baby pack, wishing again it went on my chest instead of my back. I have visions of her falling out or being snatched by a huge and silent bird of prey or dying back there and I wouldn't know so I'd keep on trudging through the damn yellow woods with a dead baby or an empty pack on my back. She's even stiffer than usual this morning and I have to forcibly bend her tiny limbs to get her in. Her complaints are vague, part of her general distress with being in the world. "There." I kiss her soft cheek. "Ready to go see Mommy?" Her pale blue eyes don't even flicker. I don't know what I expected.

Taking more care not to jar her than is probably necessary, I slide the straps of the backpack over my shoulders and straighten to adjust the weight, though there isn't much that couldn't be accounted for by the pack itself. I crouch, slide the straps off again, gently set the pack down, with some trepidation crab-walk to inspect. She's still there. I haven't lost her yet. All the way to Emily's she makes little noises that can't be mistaken for birds or creaking branches or the gurgles of any other baby or anything but what they are.

"How is she?" I greet Earl. Poor guy, I ought to at least say good morning, but that seems too personal for the kind of relationship we have.

Busy getting the kids off to school, he looks over at Bella but doesn't speak to her or come any closer, and certainly makes no move to take her from me. "About the same," he says of his wife. His normally lean face is haggard in the yellow morning light, and his words, always few and clipped, are edgy.

"How can I help?"

"Erin can't find something. I don't know what. Every morning it's something." Sort of helplessly, he gestures toward the stairs.

"I'll go."

By the time I get to her room, Erin has found the lost homework assignment and has turned her attention to Evan, who's not dressed. They're facing off in the hallway, yelling at each other. The sight of Bella—I assume that's what it is—makes Erin retreat into her room. Awkwardly with the baby still on my back, I kneel to help Evan tie his shoes. But my ministrations seem only to make things worse. He squirms and complains until finally I give up altogether on the idea of double knots.

The fact that no one directly acknowledges Bella's presence rekindles my paranoid fantasies that she's not really among us. I see to it that Erin and Evan get themselves downstairs and then, before entering Emily's room, I take off the pack, remove the baby from it, check that she's still breathing. Like an amoeba, she recoils when I touch her. Her glassy blue eyes scan me without so much as a blip of interest. Her mouth works to no particular purpose. Her subtly abnormal little face scrunches and smoothens and stretches in what I know are no more precursors to human language than the inchoate noises that come out of her.

I stand here in the dim yellow morning light of the hallway, holding in my two hands away from my body this little creature that suggests but doesn't really approximate a human baby. For a hideous moment I want nothing more than to lay her on the grey linoleum outside her mother's bedroom door—which, I notice, is slightly ajar—and just slink away. I would lay her there gently; I wouldn't throw her or let her drop.

In the slough of that impulse, I'm not thinking about Emily or about Bella herself. It's Daddy I'm thinking about. "Fuck you," is what I'm thinking. "I'm not doing this. I don't accept your gift or curse or whatever the hell it is. Take it back, you hear me? Stick it where the sun don't shine."

The baby sways in my grasp like a sack almost but not quite empty. When I bring her in to my chest, she responds no more and no less. From the smell of her she needs a diaper change, but she, of course, isn't fussing any more or less than usual.

Using my fists and the baby's body to push open the door, I step into Emily's room. It smells of bananas, urine, sweat, strawberry-scented candles. "Emily," I say, though I don't yet see where she is. "I've brought you your daughter."

She doesn't say anything, but I hear her breathing. Then I make out her form, curled up on the floor, just outside and under a shaft of drizzly yellow light. The window is bare because the curtains have been pulled down; the rod hangs by one end, catching pale sunlight here and there along its dented surface. Noticing that rather dramatic detail leads to awareness of others: the iridescent streak of a crack across the bottom pane, the natter of a radio turned low, debris underfoot and against shins, furniture disarrayed, the overhead light illuminating nothing beyond itself at this time of day.

I take a few careful steps toward Emily, over and around things. She has wrapped herself in the curtain, and I find this particularly horrifying—so desperate and minimally functional it seems, so patently crazy.

I'm tempted to take Bella as far away as possible, but this doesn't seem a real option. Instead I cross with her through the mounds of clothes and books and food-encrusted dishes, kneel in front of her mother, my sister, make sure my one-armed grasp of the baby is firm and put my other hand on Emily's knee. "Em?"

There's not even a pause. From her crouching position she flings herself against me—awkwardly, without much force, but full out, knocking me backward and jarring the baby. The baby, in fact, grunts; this may be the first time I've observed her respond directly to any stimulus. She doesn't cry. Emily and I are crying. With Bella between us, we are in each other's arms.

Eva Marie left us forty-three years ago today. I have always marked the anniversary in some way. My children have not. Momentous as this day was in all our lives,

they have treated it with their characteristic inatten-
tiveness. Not infrequently I ask myself how these can
be my offspring.

In the early years, I would imagine her returning on
this day of all days, emerging through the yellow wood as
if she had never lived here or never been away. Sometimes
in these fantasies I would sic Herpie on her. Sometimes I
would rush to meet her and kneel at her feet, present her
with what I had been holding back from her, and then, in
a transcendent act of love and sacrifice, send her away
again. Most often I would simply be waiting.

She never came back, of course. Conjuring has never
been my game.

The tenth year, I began the book, and writing it became
my anniversary reaction. In a black spiral-bound book
the size of an infant's palm (an image which, predictably,
leads today to the image of the reflexive opening and
closing of the infant Bella's deceptively perfect hand), I
write a poem on one day every year; the preceding 364
days I will have been writing and re-writing the same
lines in my head, in a quest for perfection equally decep-
tive. I prepare now to make another entry in the poetic
narrative, perhaps the last.

All of this year's mental composition seems to have
quite missed the point. I have forgotten almost all of it;
only insipid snippets remain. At mid-morning on the
appointed day, no inspiration has struck. I have been
up since well before dawn, sitting in my chair, losing

myself in my own house in my own thoughts, wandering in the dark wood and its dim counterpart the cave, all the while fingering the ballpoint pen and tiny notebook in my pocket against my straining thigh but never once removing them to put one to the other.

Now I sit on the yellow porch, on the single metal folding chair left from a set of six, not so uncomfortable that I am willing to expend the energy to remove the sticks and leaves that have accumulated in its seat. The notebook open and still blank on my knee, I sit with my eyes closed, waiting. It is not inconceivable that Eva Marie might come this year, might come today.

Cold-blooded Herpie, adaptable to a fault, is sunning and shading herself in the green-gold at the edge of the porch. When Vaughn arrives, clattering and clanging most unmusically, Herpie hisses, Vaughn utters a childish profanity, and I tell them both to go somewhere else if they must bicker. Neither leaves, but they do settle down.

Vaughn asks me, "How are you doing, Dad?" The peculiar gentleness in his tone causes me to wonder if he does realize what day this is—he of them all. However, I do not know what, if anything, is the point of his inquiry, and rhetorical questions are a waste of time, so I do not answer.

On the upturned page of the opened notebook, someone has written "Dear Sandi." Of course it must have been I who wrote it; no one else has had access to this book. But I have no mental or kinesthetic memory of having *done so, and I think perhaps Sandi, whoever that may be, has somehow written it herself, written a salutation to herself as a prompt for me. To do what I cannot guess. It is decidedly un-poetic.*

"Emily . . . Em, are you okay? Are you going to be okay?"

She is sobbing and shaking. Her head moves against me. She smells dirty and her hair is greasy against my lips. Bella, redolent of bath powder and poop, stirs meaninglessly between us, closer to me than to her. The curtain makes a brown-and-gold tent over the three of us until my sister gathers it again around just herself.

"Sweetie, come on. You can't stay in here forever. Your husband and children need you. I need you. I came all this way to see you. I have to go home to my own husband and kids soon."

None of this makes any perceptible impression on her; to me, too, it's hopelessly scattershot. What I'm going to say next is brazen, but I'm going to say it. Holding the baby across my knee with one hand, I reach out to touch my little sister's cheek with the other. She doesn't pull away, emboldening me to let loose of Bella and take her mother's face in both my hands. "Emily. Listen to me. Bella needs you."

Emily's eyes are huge, but they do not take in her daughter wedged in my lap. She whispers something I don't understand, repeats it only slightly more loudly. "Needs what? Needs what from me?"

I'm starting to get mad now, I shake her a little. "How should I know? But she's your baby. You need to take care of her. It's not my job, Em."

When she still doesn't make any move toward Bella, I lose patience altogether, let her go with a gratuitous little shove, and none too gently grab the baby. Her mewling is like the sound of the radio—just barely audible, not quite white noise. Her neck arches dangerously under the weight of her unsupported head.

"Here!" I all but snarl. Emily recoils. "Here, goddammit, take your fucking kid!" When I throw the child at her, all three of us scream.

My other sons have appeared now, the three of them positioning themselves like a Greek chorus at what appear to be choreographed stations on the porch. Neither of my daughters is here. Why is that? Vaughn absentmindedly strums something stringed. Will carries inside my house a basket of tomatoes, their fragrance still on him when he returns. Galen speaks.

"Dad, we have to talk to you about something."

I will not discuss the deformed infant. It has no relation to me. They can do with it as they please. I make a show of writing in the notebook, though what I am inscribing there is gibberish.

Galen blusters. "Dad. Listen. Will you listen for once?"

Will wheedles. "Please, Dad. This is important. We really need you to hear what we have to tell you."

It falls to Vaughn to convey their message, in fits and starts with accompanying harmonica blasts, bell jingles, fractured drum rolls. "Mom—" a swish of strings—"wants to—" a rattle of castanets—"see you."

Emily has somehow managed to break Bella's fall with her own swaddled body, and for just a moment it seems this protective instinct, whether maternal or not, is a breakthrough. I'm backing away. But she comes after me, stumbling over the curtain, crashing against the bed and dresser, knocking over a lamp, backing me against the door I haven't been able to get open in time.

She shoves herself hard against me with the baby pressed too tightly between us. Her breath reeks. When she lets go of the baby, flinging her arms wide, I have no choice but to replace her hands with my own. Bella is now howling and flailing.

Emily is howling and flailing, too, shrieking at me to get out and leave her alone and stay away and go fuck myself, throwing things. Something breaks against the wall over my head. Something small and hard bounces off my forearm, another, another. The radio suddenly blares, an assault.

Because the door opens inward, I'm forced to move toward my raging sister in order to get away from her. The knob is loose and doesn't readily turn. By the time I get out of the room, Emily has collapsed, Bella is hysterical, and something like fury propels me headlong down the stairs shouting, "Earl!"

Bella by now is nothing but her panic, which I imagine to be a sort of primal organismic response to a global threat. Her cries are guttural like something out of a bad horror movie. Her bugged-out eyes, showing more white than blue, roll from side to side and up and down and even back into her head. Her body contorts with a strength that seems preternatural, limbs spinning and striking out, torso arching backward and then forward so forcibly she almost sits up. Her head lolls wildly as if her neck has broken.

"Earl!"

Her diaper overflows, yellowish liquid shit dripping onto the floor as I hold her precariously away from me.

"Goddammit! Earl! Erin! Eli! Evan!"

Everybody else has left. I charge around the house shouting every E-name except Emily's, but nobody other than Emily is here, and she's not about to take this feral little creature off my hands. Nor would I allow her to.

My increasingly reckless trajectory finally takes me out of the house altogether and into the wet yellow wood, toward the house of my father, who in one way or another is at the root of all this insanity because he is at the root of everything. I will not do this. I will not accept this. Fuck you, Daddy, you can't make me do this anymore.

Chapter 10

Here she comes now, long strong stride bringing her out of the yellow wood. In her arms she cradles an infant, so close against her breast I fear for them both. Evidently Eva Marie is willing to take the risk, which I understand and laud for the very reason that such passionate protectiveness is quite outside my personal repertoire. When we were together it was outside hers as well. This is how I failed her. She was forced to leave us in order to learn to love.

No, this is not Eva Marie. Eva Marie has not returned this year any more than any other year. This is some other woman, some other infant, mewling. Alexandra.

My brothers are arrayed like ridiculous toy soldiers on the dank porch of my father's house. Daddy's among them; I can see his bent knees. I'm yelling before I get there. "Hey, assholes, come help me with this baby! She's your niece, too!" It's a lot to yell, and no doubt incomprehensible to them, but I'm on a roll and I keep yelling. "Get your ass out here and take her! She's your granddaughter!"

Vaughn drifts toward me then gets distracted—I suppose by his own music—and drifts off, trailing drumbeats and autoharp chords. Galen and Will stay where they are. Daddy gets stiffly to his feet, tucks something into the hip pocket of his awful plaid pants, and leaves the porch by the opposite end without acknowledging my presence or Bella's. Why am I not surprised.

"Well, shit," says Will, wearily, the way he says everything.

In my hands Bella has stopped writhing, but she's still producing that hoarse gulping sound that abruptly I can't stand one more minute. Less to comfort than to silence her, I pull her into me, press her face against my chest. The sound is muffled but not stopped so she must still be breathing. The ubiquitous Herpie slithers insolently under my feet, as if I wouldn't dare step right on her, and disappears into the knee-high yellow weeds around the porch.

The drizzle has thickened into downright rain. I tent the baby's head with my palm but—stubbornly, I guess, or maybe wisely—don't step up onto the porch where we'd both be sheltered. "I'm not doing this! You hear me? I'm not doing this all by myself. I resign."

"Oh, get over yourself." That's Galen. I want to smash his face.

"It's fucking raining. One of you has got to take this baby."

Galen says, "Hey. Watch your language. We don't talk like that around here." We are all so predictable.

Predictably, I lower my voice to what I hope is a menacing growl. "Will. Take her in the house. Now."

He hesitates, but never one to refuse an order, direct or inferred from the strongest personality around him at any given moment, he comes to the edge of the porch and reaches down. Rain slithers and hisses between us. I hand the hiccuping infant up and over to him. Rain is now dripping off my hair and soaking the shoulders and the back of my T-shirt. My hands and the baby's face look yellow.

Will starts wordlessly into the house with her, but I've climbed onto the porch—predictably, from the long side where there are no steps; might as well make this as hard as possible. Shrugging out of the pack, I'm telling him to wait, she needs a diaper change.

"Great. Thanks a lot."

"I'll feed her in a few minutes. Don't you try it. She has a lot of trouble swallowing. Sometimes she chokes. They're probably going to put in a feeding tube, just to keep her alive."

Will looks down at Bella. "Um," he says, as if to her, "okay."

"There are clothes in there, too, if she's wet. If they aren't damp from the rain."

"Okay."

Then he just stands there, looking bewildered. Out of pity, maybe, I make a clumsy overture. "I bet you're glad to see this rain, aren't you? Good for the garden. Martin always celebrates rain."

Right away I realize my *faux pas*. Having lived for so long in a semi-arid climate, I forgot for a moment where I am now. Will's face animates darkly. "Everything's about to drown or wash away. So, yeah, maybe I ought to be celebrating." I don't know what to say. Desolately he glares out at the rain, which is heavy by now, and then takes the baby into the house.

I turn on my oldest brother and demand, "Okay, Galen, what the fuck is going on around here?"

It's a sort of all-purpose challenge, and I don't exactly know what response I'm going for, but it sure as hell isn't the one I get. He squares his shoulders and directly meets my gaze to tell me, "Mom's here."

Although I have lived my entire life in yellow humidity, I dislike it. I dislike the soggy ground, the mist and rivulets dirtying my glasses, my shirt adhering to my back, the dank smell.

Herpie crawls gamely through the mud and wet brambles. My shoes slip and stick. Every branch I grasp for balance is too pliable from moisture to be of any use and only streams cold rain and leaves upon me. Unprotected by hair or hat, my scalp cringes from the chill, and my head aches.

The reason for haste has slipped my mind—what the object might be, whether I am escaping or pursuing—but this does not diminish the need for haste. Working my left hand into my hip pocket, I find it damp and empty. Panic seizes me, but when I think to check my right pocket the small notebook is safe, neither lost nor ruined by rain.

Often, though less frequently as years went by, Eva Marie and I wandered through this wood in rain, as well as in fog and moonlight and darkness, twilight and dawn and rare dappled midday sunshine. At first these were not romantic interludes or episodes of any other sort of intimacy. I would keep my hands in my pockets, or occupied with tools, or clasped behind my back. I would stay paces ahead of her or paces behind. We seldom talked, and our silences, though I think not hostile, were also not often especially companionable.

"I'm scared," she would say nearly every time, shouting or whispering or in irritating baby talk. "These woods are creepy. I don't like being out here in these woods, Alexander. Alex, please, I want to go home. Let's go home."

For innumerable reasons—temperament, childhood training, weak character—both Eva Marie and I were afraid of many things. Each other. Our children. People in any way unlike ourselves, which meant all people. Social situations. Artistic self-expression; she had a real feel for colour and texture and design, occasionally would go so far as to buy fabric and thread, but as far as I know never finished a piece. Travel. Friendship. Love in any form.

When Eva Marie was pregnant with our first child, I took her to the hideout I had discovered not long before, even more recently made usable for purposes which at that time were still unclear. She resisted. She wept. She claimed sickness, fatigue, pain, swollen ankles, concern for the foetus. I persisted, led her to the grotto under the granite outcropping. At the sight of Herpie stretched out in the line of pale sunshine at the edge of the rock, she screamed and fluttered her hands. I took her by the shoulders and pressed her down onto her knees, though she cried out about the mud on her white maternity slacks. I urged her into the dim cave and settled her in what was then her place. At the time I had no reservations about being a bully, and I have no regrets about that now, only that I did not persevere.

She made unseemly sexual advances to which I could not prevent myself from responding, although to do so was against my intent, my better judgment, and my will. I was a young man, with the woman I loved, however guardedly, in a low-lit, secluded place. She distracted me, and I succumbed.

For a while then, I tested the theory that sex might be a way of transferring to my wife—ejaculating into her, if you will—this most vital of aptitudes. This was not self-indulgence, as Eva Marie believed; I was at least as uncomfortable with what I was proposing as she was. She said I made her feel like a whore. I saw it as a failure of nerve on both our parts. When that phase ended, having veered close to pornography and produced no beneficial results, we could scarcely look at each other, did not touch each other for a long time, and both considered ourselves to have been vindicated in our instinctive stance against the risks of physical passion and, by extension, passion in any form.

I did make several other attempts at presenting to Eva Marie what I knew to be essential to the world but could not myself put into practice: the ability and the willingness to love large and deeply. I saw how we were with Galen, and then with the other children, one after another. Both of us loved them, in our own fashion—which is to say, not very well. Neither of us could say it or show it directly, or, in truth, feel it with any real conviction. It was too much to ask—it has always been too much to ask—for me to love like that, but had I been sufficiently strong and skilled and daring, had I used the powers I was beginning to recognize, I believe I could have given it to Eva Marie. And then she would not have left.

Eva Marie became increasingly constricted. She did little but tend to the children's basic needs, and that without much enthusiasm. She was hardly sleeping or eating; her eyes hollowed and her skin dulled. More and more real and fantasized dangers paralyzed her—she admitted to snakes, falling trees, kidnappers, other children carrying disease, touching me, talking with me, living with me, caring for our children, the wood at night, the wood in rain, the sunlit wood. She would hardly leave the house. Soon she would not leave the house at all.

The wood is now filled with rain. Rain grows among the trees. The noise of rain among trees is deafening. I am cold. I have been told of, or have concocted, Eva Marie's summons; she wants to see me, but I do not know where she is. I might almost be floating. I might almost be drowning.

Emily was a colicky baby. For the first ten months of her life, she screamed almost constantly. We had four other small, demanding children. When not at my quiet job at the county library, I was spending a great deal of time in the cave, justifying this behaviour to myself— and not without reason, I still maintain—by working on methods of infusing Eva Marie with the ability to rear these children in more than a cursory, obligatory manner. I had fundamental doubts as to my own ability in that regard, but continued to believe I could discover a way of giving it to her.

At various times, certain potions seemed to show promise; I have notes, but looking them up would be pointless. I was also experimenting with mixtures, sequences, juxtapositions of ancient and otherwise traditional incantations, as well as composing originals; notebooks filled with annotated drafts are still extant, utterly irrelevant now.

Our children provided practice opportunities and heightened my awareness of all that was insufficiently good and loving and steadfast and beautiful in the world into which they had been born. Galen was not yet four years old the first time I took him to the cave. An exuberant boy then, he paid little attention to either his mother's dutiful protests or her distracted relief; with a two-year-old and a newborn, she was decidedly unfocused, easy for both of us to ignore. When we left the house, she was weeping, Will was shrieking and banging on the tray of his high chair where he had probably been left too long, Vaughn was wailing in his crib, and although it was not raining the wood dripped grey-yellow under a low grey sky.

In a thick new notebook I had worked out a plan, a sort of experimental design, beginning with a rather lengthy list of qualities I considered deficient in the world but was myself incapable of putting into action. Doubting I would have enough children for all the items, I had been forced to combine and prioritize.

Having chosen with this firstborn son to begin with social responsibility, high on my list, I had worked out a careful protocol. Galen noticed the gun, of course, and begged to be allowed to hold it. Of course I refused. He regarded it curiously. "What's it do, Daddy?"

"It's a hunting rifle. It kills animals."

His eyes widened. "Why?"

"For fun."

He took that in, nodded, crouched to examine some interesting stone or leaf or ball of dirt. I called him to me and we continued our trek until we reached the cave, by which he was immediately fascinated, as I had known he would be.

However, he was afraid to enter, so I crawled in first, laid the rifle in its predetermined place, then turned and beckoned; holding out my arms to him would have been better, but beckoning was the best I could do. I saw the courage it took for him to follow my orders. Sympathy made me brusque. "Do not dawdle," I told him. "We have no time for dilly-dallying."

Settled awkwardly on my lap, he began asking a four-year-old's endless questions about everything in his field of perception, from cave walls to Herpie to sounds from the wood to the array of envelopes and Mason jars he spotted in the back corner. "What's that, Daddy? Why's it called that? What's it do? Why's it do that? Can I have it? Does it like me? Is it yours? Is it your friend? What's that?" To many such questions there are no known answers. I provided him with a few—though not all—of those I had, but he was not satisfied, and I quickly became impatient as ever with slow, incremental, unpredictable teaching.

Mentally checking off the steps I had outlined in the notebook, I set Galen off my lap, to his mild objections. I took up the vial of blue-green liquid and the pouch of grey powder I had prepared just that morning for maximum freshness and strength. The risk was undeniably sobering.

I had researched thoroughly, but these alchemical con-coctions are drawn from materials rife with metaphor and innuendo impossible to verify, and I had added my own touches. Though I had exercised as much caution as I could bring to bear, it was still not inconceivable that I was about to cause great harm to my son. Hoping with grim fervour that this would not be the case, I nonetheless had no doubt that the risk was justified by the potential benefit to him and to humanity.

Allowing Galen to continue his prattling, I mixed the powder into the liquid, which in appearance and taste somewhat resembled Kool-Aid of an unknown flavour. He heard the clink of the spoon and twisted around to look. "What's that, Daddy? Can I have some?"

"Yes, son, you may have some. But first I want to show you something." Because I then put one arm around him, he both saw and felt me raise the gun. Perhaps he heard it as well, the dull rattle of metal and wood against flesh. Perhaps he smelled it.

This was one of Herpie's first assignments from me, and she performed well. On cue, a brown rabbit with a frantic white tail hopped across the narrow vista framed by the cave opening, Herpie in silent, invisible pursuit. I felt Galen's little gasp just before I pulled the trigger. The rabbit screamed, spasmed, spurted blood, fell.

The echo was still ricocheting around us as I laid the gun behind me out of Galen's reach, held the elixir to his lips, tilted his head back, and commanded, "Now swallow." Stunned, he opened his mouth. Almost play-fully, his cheeks stayed ballooned for a few moments. Then he swallowed.

Despite my efforts at preparing myself not to expect immediate results, I began almost at once to despair. Galen showed no effect at all. He took the potion willingly enough, and when it was gone he licked his lips, wiped his mouth with the grimy back of his hand, pulled me by the sleeve to go look at the dead rabbit. The creature lay in the weeds, contorted and bloody, one eye staring. "Is the bunny sick, Daddy?"

"It is dead, son."

"What's 'dead'?"

"Dead is no longer alive." Unhelpful, I could see, but accurate.

"Oh." Abruptly he whooped and jumped over the mess, as if it were a hurdle in a game, and before I could stop him had stuffed a handful of juniper berries into his mouth. I reached him in time to force him to spit them out and to swat his bottom for disobeying the rule about not eating things from the wood without parental approval, which meant my approval because Eva Marie claimed inability to distinguish poisonous from healthful. His distress was so short-lived I doubted the punishment had been effective, but out of concern for the experiment I did not administer more. We went home.

That night amid the cacophony of supper, from which I always did my best mentally to absent myself, Galen suddenly announced to his mother, "My Daddy did a bad thing."

Preoccupied as always, Eva Marie paid him no heed. Galen raised his voice and the stakes. "My Daddy's a bad man."

This time Eva Marie did glance up, but at that moment Will spilled something and the baby spat up, and she shouted at them both. Through the din I pressed Galen. "What bad thing did I do?"

He was still looking at his mother, but he said to me, "You killed that bunny dead."

By reminding myself of the importance of what I was trying to do, that this cause was much bigger than my personal relationship with my son, I was able to triumph over the impulse to defend my actions. "And why is that bad?"

He stared, not so much at me as off into some internal distance. Eva Marie and the two younger boys were escalating, and there was not much time before I would be forced to intervene. I waited. Galen waited. Then his eyes cleared and he climbed onto his chair. He waved his fork like a flag and proclaimed, "That bunny has as much right to live as you do!"

This was not the syntax of a four-year-old. "Right to live" was not a child's concept. I had no doubt something new had been instilled in him. As I got up to rescue Will from his mother, I said to my eldest son, "Good boy, Galen. Good job," and his face glowed.

Over the next months I carefully built upon that first step, with more visits to the cave, more elixirs and emollients, a few small rituals with fire and water and certain words of my own composition. By the time Galen entered kindergarten, he was ready to lecture the other children about animal rights, to be the designated caretaker of the classroom pets, to achieve a certain fame for his precocious commitment to the greater good. Even people who did not agree with him—and in our district the schools were closed on the first days of doe and buck season—took note of his ardour and ability to express it, and a few told us he had changed their attitudes.

But I did not intend for him to stop there. Killing a rabbit before the eyes of a four-year-old had been the easiest route I could think of into his psyche, but there were many other important social causes. We continued our work.

In third grade, Galen spearheaded a fund drive at his school for a local family whose house had burned; I myself could never ask people for money. At the age of eleven, he was collecting signatures on petitions to decrease federal defence spending; I had explained to him at some length the immorality of war in terms a boy his age could understand while he chewed a certain efficacious gum. By the time he entered junior high he had rallied for peace and civil rights, and in high school he led a delegation to the Mock U.N. where his team took first place.

When he came home I would be waiting to hear all about it. I was very proud, and very watchful. Now and

179

then he would protest, mount a short-lived resistance to ingesting what I gave him, or otherwise resist, but without much passion or stamina.

To my satisfaction, Galen continued his social and political activities well into middle adulthood. He was an activist against the Vietnam and Gulf Wars despite this area's simple-minded patriotism. He was successful, at least for the time being, in thwarting efforts to develop the southeast quadrant of the wood into a housing tract, even though he did not seem fully convinced of his own position. I applauded, silently, his skill and commitment which allowed me to effect social change by proxy. At the same time, I chafed. I could do more.

Now that he has married, Galen is obviously weary of his role. He would not say so directly, but he does not want to be away from his wife. He has no interest anymore in large-scale social action. He merely wishes to nest. And the time is long past when I might have had more direct access to his psyche.

There is, however, no dearth of worthy causes someone in this family must address. I maintain a list. Through Galen's agency, the Koves have been a force for the greater good, and we will continue to be.

Will's gardening and Vaughn's music were easy enough to impart. Will was and is simple-minded in a more literal sense than the term usually implies—not unintelligent, but also not complex or deep or difficult to penetrate. I worked the soil with him a few times, demonstrated to

him the wonders of germination and photosynthesis—
processes that I understand but do not experience as
wonderful—and tamped the gift into place in his spirit
with a simple, well-placed chant; he has not been free
of it since.

Vaughn's psyche was characterized from a very early
age by high degrees of both suggestibility and obses-
siveness. Therefore, that particular transference (I say
"transference" in this case because I did once have a
musical bent and still listen to the classics because it
is a worthwhile activity, although anything that could
be termed enjoyment has long since faded) perhaps
would have required only a single sprinkling of rarefied
singing stone to lock in his natural aptitude with the
natural aptitude of the music itself. However, I decided
to test the injection technique, by this time developed
and refined to a limited degree. On two occasions, once
in his bedroom when his older brothers were at school
and once in a misty yellow clearing, I filled myself with
the imagined need and ability to create music, as fully
imagined as I could tolerate, and then shot it into him.
Back then, I required physical contact. My son and I sat
facing each other, on the Mickey Mouse rug and again
on the damp yellow ground, and I held his head in my
hands, pressed his temples with my fingertips and his
eyelids with my thumbs. At first it was a game to him.
Very soon it was not. I was stronger than he and did
not let him go until the transfer was as complete as my

power and stamina—considerable at that time in my life—would support.

Earl has more to do with Emily's fecundity than I. However, having missed the opportunity with her mother, I blessed and cursed her with a devotion to parenthood that has worked well for her and for her children. Until now, until this child who can scarcely be called a human child. I have no spells or magic substances for this, nor do I have the energy or fortitude to concoct any. I am too weary to try to imagine what claiming a child like this would be. I am used up. This is asking too much.

Seeing Eva Marie after all this time is asking too much. Not seeing her when she is close by and has asked for me is unthinkable.

I am soaked to the skin and shivering. Every joint in my body protests. I have come to a fork in the path. One direction seems more worn than the other, though in the driving rain I may be misperceiving. As is my wont, I take the more travelled route.

Cognitively, it doesn't even compute at first, but I have an immediate visceral reaction—chills, tingling, ringing in my ears. Gaping stupidly, I manage, "Mom? Here? Here at the house?"

"She's at Vaughn's."

"At *Vaughn's*?" The thought of my mother—I couldn't say the image, since I have no current mental picture of her—in my youngest brother's decrepit one-and-a-half-room cabin, among the clutter of musical instruments and dirty clothes and pop cans, is so grotesque it makes me laugh. "You mean you guys have been in touch with her all these years? All of you have? I'm the only one who hasn't?"

"You weren't around, now were you, Alexandra."

Emerging from the house with Bella, Will is kinder. "Not all these years. She contacted us when she was diagnosed."

"Diagnosed with what?" Not that the name of it matters.

"Some kind of heart thing. She says she doesn't have long. She wanted to see us."

Galen corrects him. "She wanted to see Dad."

"How long has she been here?"

"A week or so."

"A *week*? And you didn't think to mention it to me?"

"You didn't seem all that interested."

"Fuck you. Does Daddy know she's here?"

"He didn't until a few minutes ago."

"He didn't *know*? How could he not know?" My brothers shrug and shake their heads and look away. After a while I breathe, "Jesus fucking Christ."

"She wants to see you, Alexandra." This is Galen, of course, setting up the moral order.

"Not a chance in hell."

"She's your mother."

"In name only."

"You owe her—"

"I owe her nothing."

"This may be your last chance."

"Good."

"Sandi."

"Anyway, that's what you said about Daddy to get me here." I'm shaking.

"And it was the truth."

"While you're here," Will points out, wanly cheerful. "Kill two birds."

The turn of phrase makes me snort, offending both Galen and Will for different reasons. "Where is Daddy anyway?"

"Who knows?"

Returning the baby to me, Will says, "Think about it, Sandi. Will you at least think about it?"

"Like I'll be thinking about anything else, you idiot."

Galen issues orders. "Be here at five o'clock. We'll take you to see her. All of us. Emily, too."

"Emily won't leave the house. Emily won't leave her *room*."

"Oh, she will." Promise or threat, this declaration isn't hollow.

I make a declaration of my own. "I'm not doing it, Galen."

Without even exchanging a glance, my brothers have formed a two-person phalanx and started moving out into the woods, presumably to find our father.

"No way!" I shout after them, clutching the baby. "You hear me? No fucking way!" In my arms Bella stiffens and then goes limp, panting and rolling her big blue eyes.

Chapter 11

At 4:45, fifteen minutes before the appointed time, I'm ready, whatever "ready" could possibly mean under these circumstances.

I've regarded myself in a mirror half a dozen times, trying to imagine how my mother will see me, how I want her to see me, whether and why I care. I look fat. I look old. I look sturdy and solid. Humidity makes it another bad hair day. The blue shirt and black jeans look good. There's no resemblance to the seven-year-old she left behind.

I've called home twice, both times got voice mail, hung up without leaving a message. Home—that home—seems not so much distant in time and space as stowed for safekeeping.

I've tried to think what I'll say to her. She's old, reputedly ill. She's a stranger, and my long-lost mother. I'm her abandoned child, and a woman well into middle age—which is to say, with much less than half my life to live. My children have been abandoned, too, though not—I hope—by me. Somehow I am not only the aunt but also the guardian of this unreachable baby Bella, her unreachable granddaughter. If she and I have any current link, it's through Alexander Kove.

That's the best I can do. I don't know how to think about any of this.

At 4:55, Will and Galen tromp into the house and announce they haven't found Daddy. Emily is with them, pale and shaky but more or less dressed and moving more or less under her own power. I start to go to her but she backs away, from me or from her child in my arms. Abruptly past my limit with her, I fix her with my best disapproving glare. Not looking at my brothers, I demand of them, "Should we worry about him? Should we call the cops or something?" Galen snorts.

"I bet he's with Mom," Will offers, and in fact this preposterous notion does seem the most likely among a host of utterly unlikely scenarios.

Bella squalls for no apparent reason. It's by no means the first time I've heard her make this cry, different from that of a normal infant in some subtle, creepy way. Emily flinches and hugs herself. When the noise has run its course, the baby's mouth stays open, copiously drooling.

Galen commands, "Let's go," and the whole wildly dysfunctional band of us troops off through the goddamn yellow wood. At the moment, no actual precipitation is penetrating the leaf canopy, but everything is dripping and the sky is so low it's like a sodden web down here among us, among the trees. On my shoulder, Bella whimpers, and of course I don't know why.

Deliberately I formulate thoughts of my husband and children. Right about now, Martin should be getting home from work and Ramon would have just left for the restaurant—if he's on the schedule for tonight; if he's even still working there. It unnerves me that I don't know that, or how Martin's day might have been, or whether he's taking Tara out for dinner tonight or they're ordering in pizza or one or the other of them is cooking, that I'm not up to date with the details of my daughter's summer vacation: Does she have any friends? Is she watching too much TV? Are her allergies kicking up? It unnerves me even more that I'm fumbling for details. I miss them, but in such a non-specific way it's not much more than theoretical.

With even less success, I try to think about work. Have I missed any deadlines? How much longer will I be able to cobble together telecommuting and email conferencing and what's left of my family leave? Beyond a vague anxiety, I can't even bring myself to care.

Bella squirms against my shoulder. Herpie makes a rivulet through the yellow-brown leaf mulch. My

brothers and sister and I march in age-old forma-
tion through the woods in search of our parents.
Music I can't help thinking of as yellow, though
that's nonsense, keens very softly, the music of the
goddamn spheres.

*A cabin emerges from the sodden, faintly yellow wood,
surreal although I know perfectly well it is Vaughn's cabin
and I have been here before. I know this. Harmonica music
fountains out of it, simultaneously rollicking and mourn-
ful as only harmonica music can be—cabin, music, wood,
all of a piece. Something—a snake; Herpie—swishes
through the underbrush just behind or just ahead of me,
peculiarly audible, setting off little sprays of water drop-
lets like sparks. Wondering what Herpie has in mind, I
chide myself for the persistence of the anthropomorph-
izing habit. The music draws me. I am somewhat lost in
the self-perpetuating forward motion of my own bent
body, stumbling feet, mind and spirit overfull. The music
fades and stops.*

Eva Marie opens the door.

*Someone opens the door. An old woman. Confused
and alarmed, I stop. My clothes are wet. Trees and the
cabin's ragged roofline drip vertiginous yellow. The door,
which has been opened, opens farther.*

"Alexander," she calls. Eva Marie calls my name. "Alex!"

*I cannot do this. It is asking too much. Although it is
the right and necessary thing to do, it is well beyond my*

capacity. I must designate a representative, a surrogate.
   Alexandra, of course. Alexandra must do this for me.
For all of us.

Behind me, Emily gasps. Will exclaims her name, and I look over my shoulder and over the baby's lolling head to see my sister on the ground and my brother grasping her arm in a misguided attempt at assistance that twists her head and torso into what looks like a painful angle. Galen pivots, pushes past me to help Will get Emily to her feet. It figures that Galen would be one of those people whose idea of righting a situation is to get someone upright, no matter what's wrong with them.

I turn and keep walking. Too late, I realize Bella and I have been manoeuvred to the head of the procession. No one tells me to wait. I suppose they're all following in one way or another, but the sounds from back there are garbled and the path has become too slippery and overgrown for me to risk another backward glance. The responsibility of carrying this baby is huge and inchoate. The responsibility of dealing with my mother—*my mother*—is more than I ever signed up for. What I find myself fiercely thinking is: No. Forget it. You can't make me do this. Leave me the fuck alone.

Around me, the woods hiss. Insects after rain, maybe, or sodden branches sliding against each other, or an insinuating voice—it's a sound both ominous and arousing. Bella pees and poops into an already full diaper then spits up, so now I'm splotched with a variety of excretions out of this spasming little body. My shoes catch in mud and sticky wet brush. This short trek to my brother's house in the woods has taken on epic proportions. I'm tired. I'm not even sure I'm going in the right direction, but nobody tells me otherwise.

I hear Vaughn's cabin before I see it, the wail and rollick of a harmonica playing a song I for some reason try hard to identify but can't. I yearn to sing along. I put a little dance in my step, gently bouncing Bella in time. Obviously, I'm losing my mind.

The cabin materializes out of the wood. I haven't rounded any bend in the path, and there's no obvious clearing. It's just there now where I swear it wasn't an instant ago, small and rundown, grey tinged yellow.

My father is approaching from an intersecting angle. I should have expected that. We don't hail each other. He may not even know I'm here. I don't believe that for a minute. In one way or another, he always knows where I am.

Someone opens the door, and the music stops. I have to forcibly remind myself that the almost translucent person who opens the door and raggedly calls my name is my mother. "Alexandra."

"Hello, Eva Marie."

I don't know what to call her. Any maternal name sticks in my throat. Before I can bring myself to take her extended hand, she's let it drop, as if it's too heavy for her to hold up. A cannula in her nose is connected to the plastic tubing on a tall, green, torpedo-shaped oxygen tank on wheels. I just stand there, feeling stupid, feeling helpless and trapped and tricked, but more than anything else feeling afraid. I reposition the baby from my shoulder to my chest, where her body heat can seep into me. It takes both hands to support her as she twitches and flails. Thus shielded and occupied, I say to my mother, "I didn't know you were here."

"I didn't know you were here, either." Although it's weak and shaky, it's obviously a retort. Nothing about the creaky voice evokes any shred of memory.

"Eva Marie," my father repeats. "Eva Marie."

But it's me he's looking at, and now I'm aware of him messing with my mind. Oh, no you don't. Not this time, you old bastard. Not anymore. I'm not taking any more of this shit. No way.

But I'm the one who goes to her and takes her in my arms. Because Daddy wants me to. Because Daddy gives it to me to do.

She's probably as tall as I am, but very thin, and now I can feel as well as hear her laboured breathing. Pressed between us, the baby should struggle; she

doesn't, but her presence gives me an excuse to dis-
engage quickly, which feels infuriatingly like an act
of adolescent rebellion. "Somebody take her," I hiss
at my siblings. At first nobody moves and the baby
dangles from my hands.

Finally it's Will who steps up. To our mother he
says, "I brought you some tomatoes," and he presents her with a basket I hadn't noticed him carrying.
Hands thus freed, he reaches out for Bella. Surprised
and displeased by my own trepidation, I cautiously
pass her to him, reluctant to let her go, relieved and
bereft when I do.

I don't much want to go into the cabin, either, but
everybody else is moving in that direction, including
Will, with Bella now snug in his arms. Resisting the
twin urges to scurry after him and to escape altogether, I summon the wherewithal to stay where I
am until they've all gone ahead of me.

When my father shuffles past me, to all outward
appearances a frail and befuddled old man, he raises
his wizard's eyes to mine and something streams
from his will into mine. This time he's not even being
subtle; he must be desperate, or desperately tired.
Steeling myself, I hold his gaze until he lowers his
head to navigate Vaughn's uneven threshold, but
the sensation of being injected with a hot, viscous,
mind-altering substance doesn't stop, is not depend-
ent on any other connection between us. I should

have known that; he's never had to be anywhere in my physical proximity to bless and curse me with his "gifts."

"I'm doing it, Daddy," I all but say aloud. "I'm loving Bella for the whole family, okay? What more do you want from me?"

Vaughn's not here. For some reason this makes me even more uneasy and suspicious. "Where's Vaughn?"

She—our mother—says, "I don't know. He hasn't been here all day."

She's lying—who knows why. The venom I've been hoarding for most of my life comes in handy now. "Don't give me that crap. He was just here. I heard him playing his fucking harmonica."

"Alexandra!" That's Galen, on cue. On cue, I flip him off.

"That was me," says our mother.

Emily looks at me, the first time I've seen her look directly at anybody since the baby was born. "Oh, please," I say, stupidly. "It was Vaughn. You never played the harmonica. Daddy did, and he taught Vaughn."

From the pocket of her pink pants she extracts, in fact, a harmonica. Her dark eyes flicker back and forth between my sister and me as she plays a few mournfully rollicking phrases of "Red River Valley" before a protracted coughing fit interrupts. Both actions, the playing of the harmonica and the coughing, save me from having to continue with this ridiculous argument. We all wait helplessly while the phlegmy hacking goes on and on. Embarrassed, I hate her for embarrassing me. She seems to shrink and age as she leans against the wall and then sinks into one of Vaughn's rickety chairs, the harmonica inert now in her shaking hands. Bella moans, whether in response to the music or the coughing or out of some private distress of her own, or, most likely, for no reason at all. Will strokes her misshapen head. I want to snarl at him that that won't do any good. I want to get out of here with or without her. I stand just inside the door and don't let it close behind me.

The coughing subsides. Our mother wipes at her eyes and mouth, then issues a weak, absurd invitation to all of us. "Sit down, make yourselves at home."

Emily, Daddy, and Will find chairs. Galen leans against the wall like a bouncer, arms across his chest. At a loss, I finally settle onto the floor, awkwardly cross-legged.

Then, interminably, nobody says anything. I can't stand it. To keep myself from filling the silence with something, anything, I start composing meaningful and wildly unrealistic dialogue in my head:

"Here's a sonata I wrote about the Kove family gift and curse." That would be Vaughn, who in real life would never think let alone say such a thing.

"I brought you some flowers from my garden," is what I put in Will's mouth, "and some special herbs. Here, have some. Be careful, though—they could be poisonous."

And Galen: "Peace. Justice. Social equality. It all starts here."

And Emily: "Give me my child."

Not a skilled enough writer even to imagine what my mother or Daddy or I myself might say, I'm abruptly done with this game. "So," I ask brightly, "what's new?"

My mother assumes I'm talking to her, which I guess I am, or else she just automatically keeps the chatter going. "Oh, not much. And you?"

Sitting on this uncomfortable and unstable folding chair in a room not my own among people I know both more and less than I can tolerate, aware of pain in my body and confusion in my mind and profound pervasive fatigue, knowing that forces are gathering which I might put to use if I can gather my own contrapuntal forces quickly enough—what preoccupies me is an incident between myself and Eva Marie many, many years ago, which in retrospect shows itself to have been pivotal. I wonder whether she is remembering it as well, whether in any real sense we share or shared this moment.

Although I have long been resigned to the fact that telepathy is not one of my talents, there was a time when I mistook my power to transfer patterns of thought and perception for the ability to send and receive specific thoughts. Again now, I briefly indulge myself in the fantasy that I might be able to read this woman's mind. I cannot, of course. I have no idea what she is thinking, what she wants, what she is remembering or planning. I have never had any such idea, about her or about anyone else.

But my memory of what happened between us nearly half a century ago is considerably more compelling than this current inanity. I see no reason to resist immersing myself in it.

It was an afternoon, and I was not at work, so perhaps it was a weekend or holiday, or perhaps I had taken a vacation day or called in sick. I was, in fact, sick, though no conventional physician would have confirmed my malady or malaise. What troubled me was the apprehension that something was seriously troubling my wife and that I could ameliorate, if not her distress itself, at least the disastrous results I anticipated. As it has turned out, I was quite correct in this premonition of disaster, even though clairvoyance has also never been one of my powers, which are nothing if not highly specialized, not to say rarefied.

I was in my studio under the rock ledge, working feverishly but with little focus, when Eva Marie appeared at the entrance. We had five small children. Only now, in long retrospect, does it occur to me that she must have left them alone.

The intense yellow of the wood in this memory is most likely the result of hindsight and poetic license. It is possible, however, that some suspicion on my part that this was a crucial encounter served to intensify the colour in which it occurred. Or perhaps the wood was, in fact, especially yellow that day, in response to me or for some reason of its own, illuminated by a confluence of meteorological and botanic forces.

Herpie was present. I remember noticing the golden patina of her duff-brown scales. But if she has any influence over the colour of the environment in which the two of us work, I have never observed it.

Eva Marie said to me then, "Alexander, I'm dying."

"I'm dying," my mother says now.

I think but don't say, "Well, duh. You're eighty— what? Eighty-one or something?" Chills are racing through me, and I want Bella, but across the crowded room Will is holding her fast, her head lolling against his chest, his head bowed over her.

I did not at first understand that Eva Marie was waxing metaphorical, hyperbolic, which is to say deceitful. She was not in fact dying. All these years later she is still alive, and she is saying it again, the declaration she used then as an excuse and a farewell and is using now as a salutation.

I came out of the cave to meet her in the wood itself. I believe I held out my hands to her and she refused or ignored my invitation. I demanded the clarification to which I had every right. "What do you mean? What is it?"

"What do you mean?" It's Emily who asks, Emily who as far as I know hasn't uttered a complete sentence since Bella was born, other than to curse at me. I'm incensed that our mother should be the one to get through to her.

Eva Marie's preternatural calm was disorienting. She stood just out of my reach, face in lacy leaf shadow, hands at her sides with fists unclenched. "I'm dying," she repeated, as if she had prepared no other explanation, as if that ought to be enough. But then she did go on, calmly. "I'm dying inside."

"What do you mean?"

"I can't find myself anymore. I've lost myself. I don't feel anything. I have to leave."

"Leave?"

"I can't love these children. I can't love you, Alex, I don't love you. I have to get out of here. I have to—"

Now she was speaking rapidly, urgently, and I could interrupt her. "You have an obligation—"

She interrupted me. "I know. I can't meet it. I can't do this. I'm dying, Alex. I have to leave. I already told the kids."

I stared at her. I remember staring at her, knowing full well what I should attempt and knowing I did not have the courage. By then my practice with the children gave me a clear sense of how it would be with Eva Marie. I was not capable of the sort of dedicated parenthood to which I fervently believe all children are entitled, but I knew what it was and perhaps could have given it to Eva Marie, blessed and cursed her with the ability to find herself by sacrificing herself for the children. Our children required this. Humanity requires it. Though still crude, the protocol was by then developed sufficiently that it could have been put to use. It is really rather simple:

(1) Gather the desirable attribute into concentrated psychic form.

(2) Find a point of entry into the intended recipient. If none exists, create one, understanding that damage is unavoidable.

(3) Reopen the exit wound in the sender. Damage is, again, unavoidable.

(4) Transmit. Sustain transmission as long as possible.

(5) Repeat.

(6) Repeat.

(7) Repeat. Repeat well past comfort level of both sender and recipient—in fact, past tolerance. Repeat until recipient is saturated and sender depleted.

I believe now that I could have done this, and Eva Marie would have stayed. Instead, I succumbed to profound and reprehensible moral cowardice. Rather than extending myself, I let her go.

I was not aware of having seen her turn or move, but after a long moment she had more or less faded into the yellow miasma, and we had no contact with her for forty-six years. Until now.

Now she is saying again, "I'm dying," apparently the truth this time, and once again I cannot muster the fortitude we all require.

"What does the doctor say?" Galen asks. I'm sure he must already know; this is for the benefit of the rest of us.

"I have chronic obstructive pulmonary disease."

"COPD," Galen asserts, as if correcting her. "But you smoke."

"It calms my nerves."

After a moment, I say, "I'm very sorry to hear that you're—sick. But with all due respect, what do you expect us to do about it?"

Emily gets to her feet, catches her balance, and begins to move. Ever the solipsist, I assume she's coming toward me, and I brace myself, but she goes to Will and reclaims her baby. Just like that. I wouldn't have let her take her.

The baby gurgles and cries, no more or less randomly than ever. "Bella Bella Bella," Emily chants softly.

My mother gets up, too, and the effort sets off another coughing attack. Not waiting for it to subside, she makes her way toward my father, the oxygen tank at her heels. "Alexander," she gasps, or it could be "Alexandra."

I'm shouting now. "You left us, remember?"

"Help me." Still coughing and wheezing, she stops in front of Daddy, who is more or less looking up at her. "You're the only one who can help me do this."

Music explodes. Vaughn bursts into his own house, blowing and strumming and pounding and shaking many instruments with many parts of his body. Emily screams. Bella should scream, too, but doesn't.

Several possible courses of action occur to me in flashes. I could tackle my crazy brother, tear his instruments away from him, smash them, put an end to his music and his noise. I could just sit here and take it all in and see what happens next and write about it later or not. I could make my escape under cover of the cacophony.

I stand up, spread my arms, plant my feet, throw back my head, and sing.

Though it makes no sense at all, I swear Bella sings, too.

Chapter 12

In the past week I haven't seen either of my parents—a curiously foreshortened perspective, considering that, until this summer, I hadn't been seeing them at all. I also haven't seen Bella. That peculiar family reunion at Vaughn's place seemed at the time a turning point, or the beginning of a transition or some sort of resolution, but for me what's come of it is less of just about everything—less understanding, less peace of mind, less sense of who I am and what I'm supposed to be doing here.

I haven't talked to Martin or the kids, either. That should seem strange to me, and no doubt does to them. Martin and Tara have probably called; Daddy doesn't have an answering machine or caller ID, of course, but the phone has rung a few times.

I've been alone in the house except for a visit from each of my brothers. Galen came to inform me Daddy was with Mom and we should all leave them alone until he let us know what to do and when. I said fine.

Will brought and then stayed to cook and share tomatoes, summer squash, bell peppers, eggplant. This was motivated by self-interest more than generosity since Carol and the kids will eat so little of his harvest that, meagre as he claims it to be, most of it goes to waste or, if Galen gets to it in time, to a homeless shelter in the city. I didn't eat enough to suit him, either, but it was more than I'd eaten in days.

This morning Vaughn showed up with two wooden flutes and coaxed me into playing a clumsy duet with him. He's the one who let me know Bella's getting worse, but he couldn't or wouldn't provide details.

Emily hasn't been here. I imagine she's busy.

It's been hot and muggy, hard to sleep, hard to stay awake. Everything's teeming, myself included. I can't sit still, but I can't think of anywhere to go or much of a reason to be moving.

I could be writing. All this free time with no obligations and nobody else around, all these loose thoughts and teeming images and the persistent feeling that something is trying to insinuate itself into me, pull something out of me. But I can neither concentrate nor get myself into any sort of calm, receptive, open place. The very thought of putting words on screen or paper—not to mention working on something called *Fatherland*—sets my nerves on edge.

It's after midnight, and I've been wandering aimlessly around the house, out onto the porch, even a few steps into the close woods, which are no doubt yellow though there's not enough light for actual colour. I have the urge to go to Daddy's hideout out there under the rock, the inchoate feeling that I am "supposed" to go there and find something, receive something, learn how to do something. But common sense and self-respect win out. Daddy, if you have some message or assignment or curse or gift in mind for me, bring it on. You know where I am.

Back in the living room, I laugh at myself for defiantly sitting in my father's chair, but I sit there and feel defiant anyway. Not for long, though. I pace the kitchen, stare into the refrigerator as if something edible or poisonous might have grown in there since the last time I looked, check again that the oven's turned off. I go into and out of and into Daddy's bedroom, put off and drawn by the mildly personal sights and smells of it—not very rumpled bed, eyeglasses and drinking cup and dental adhesive symmetrically arranged on the nightstand, dusty books neat and organized by author on the dusty shelf. There's nothing in here for me, though I keep thinking there ought to be.

In my own room, the room where I'm staying, I turn on the laptop, having made no conscious decision to do so. After a while I turn it off. I pull out the

Fatherland manuscript box, thinking in a scattered sort of way that maybe I'll read through what I've written and somehow get inspired.

The top page, like a cover sheet, is Frost's poem about the road not taken in the yellow wood. I didn't put it there. This is Daddy's doing, some fucking message or statement. Indignation at least has the benefit of sharpening my mental processes. He's been messing with my personal things, intending to mess with my mind.

And it's all such a crock. This may be my father's favourite poem and personal anthem, but he hasn't actually taken a road less travelled in his life. He's made the rest of us take them for him, be his sinecures, while he's played it safe and hidden.

I remove the page with the poem and crumple it, expecting to have uncovered the manuscript of my novel with Daddy's editorial comments all over it. Instead, I'm looking at a title page, in different ink but the same small, painfully erect block letters: HAND-BOOK. No author or any other attribution.

Insulted by the thought that he's re-titled my novel, I'm also a little sheepish—good title; wish I'd thought of it. But then I lift the page, and instead of my own typescript I find pages in Daddy's tight cursive. He has replaced my book with his.

My first impulse is to throw the whole thing away unread. My second, to make as big a mess as possible by dumping it on his bed. I consider sinking into despair or exploding into rage over the appropriation or destruction of my work, which is silly since I haven't exactly put a lot of concentrated energy into this thing over the years, and anyway, I have it all at home on disc. What I finally do, much more predictably and maybe sensibly, is carry the box into the living room, ensconce myself again in my father's chair where we used to read together every Saturday morning, and begin reading.

His undisguised intent makes me groan as if at a bad joke. "For Alexandra. I hereby pass it to you."

"I don't want it!" Saying aloud for the first time what has shaped and energized so much of my adult life is an entirely self-indulgent thing to do. I've never suspected my father of reading somebody else's thoughts, either telepathically or in the more normal and respectful ways most people do. But into the empty house in the middle of the night in the yellow wood I keep talking, getting louder and more emphatic. "Who do you think you are, anyway? You just keep your shit to yourself, you hear me? I'm not taking it anymore!"

Although there's never any doubt that I'll turn the page, I can hardly bring myself to do it, and by the time the first page of text is revealed I'm in a cold sweat.

Out of the corner of my eye I catch a wavy motion across the worn green carpet—the same carpet, I swear, that we all grew up on. "Fuck you, Herpie.

Leave me alone." Naturally, there's no reply. As far as I know, talking animals are not among the oddities of this decidedly odd family.

"Chapter One. Family History."

"Sandi."

Somebody's on the other side of the screen door, which to my knowledge has never boasted a lock. A man. Earl, carrying something. "Jesus, Earl, you scared the shit out of me. What's wrong?"

"You better take her."

He isn't coming in, so I push down the stiff footrest and struggle out of the recliner, putting the lid back on the manuscript box before I lay it on the floor as if he might snoop. When I open the door, Earl hands Bella to me. She's warm and breathing, but quite still. "What's wrong?"

"I'm afraid of what Emily might do."

"Oh, God, what—"

"Just take her, okay, Sandi? Please, can you take her? Here. Here's her stuff." He sets a flowered diaper bag—pitiably small to be containing all her stuff—on the porch just outside the door. Tall and thin and always craggy, he looks now like Ichabod Crane at his most desperate. He reaches out one long thin arm, covers the whole side of his daughter's face with a huge hand, nods to me, and goes away.

Stunned, I just stand there until Bella coughs, a delicate and terrifying little noise. "Oh, sweetie, are you cold?" We retreat into the house and I make a nest for her on the living room floor with blankets from my father's bed. While I'm getting her settled she opens her eyes, but she's not looking at me, probably not looking at anything. Kneeling, I stroke with a fingertip her tiny curled fist. It doesn't respond by opening to hold on. I kiss her cheek. Her glistening eyes are the colour of violets.

When we were together, Eva Marie habitually asked too little of me. Now she asks far too much.

I believe she is asleep. Her laboured breathing, not in the least smoothed by unconsciousness, makes a harsh music, which Vaughn has been trying to replicate or mock or appropriate for his own creative inspiration, experimenting with breathy and rattling instruments evidently of his own invention. This is most distracting.

The name Alexandra occurs and recurs to me, my daughter's name, but she is far away and out of my reach. The conviction has lodged in my mind that she is the one to do what Eva Marie wants. Doubtless this is unreasonable and presumptuous of me. I have no right; having gone so far when she was growing up that she had to escape, I am going even further now. But there is no choice. There is no one else to do what Eva Marie wants, and of course it must be done.

Eva Marie wants me to help her accept her own mortality. I cannot possibly do that. I know perfectly well how it ought to be done; I understand what is required, the contours of it, the texture and mechanics. The value of such an attitude, to the individual and to humanity, is inarguable and inestimable. But it is beyond me.

I know this about myself; I have always known it. My physical strength, emotional strength, strength of purpose, strength of character are and always have been woefully limited. In important matters I can see, with clarity and passion, what needs to be done, the right thing, the necessary thing, but I am almost never able to do it. At best, I can cause it to be done.

I know, for example, how to work for social justice, and I know what social justice is. I am utterly incapable of—repulsed by, terrified by—grass roots organizing or political activism, anything more overt than the very occasional letter to the editor, closely reasoned and likely to be ignored. My contribution to social justice has been to inculcate my son Galen with not only heightened sensitivity to the issues but also the ability and compulsion to act upon it. It is no small contribution.

From the standpoints of ecology, nutrition, and aesthetics, I prize the art and science of horticulture. Personally, however, I have neither the patience nor the aptitude to practise it. My thumbs are decidedly not green. My contribution to my family's health and the ozone layer has been to instil in my son Will an obsession for gardening. He struggles; he dislikes the activity and is, in fact, not nearly as expert as I had hoped, a constant source of disappointment to us both. His harvest is small, some years downright meagre. But because of his efforts—and by extension, because of mine—there is always a garden in our part of the yellow wood, and that gives me some satisfaction.

For the good of the individual psyche and the good of humanity as a whole, music must be loved. I cannot say I love music, but I appreciate it, appreciate that it must be loved. Music must continually be created in this world. I understand how to compose and to play music, but have not an iota of talent for or interest in doing so. I have given it to my son Vaughn. Through his eccentric, unfocused, but considerable talent, I make an ongoing contribution to the reservoir of music available to us all. It would be better if I were to do it myself. This is the best I can do.

Human ontogeny and phylogeny being what they are, human young being so needy and vulnerable for such a long time, parents are required to dedicate themselves to their children. They must love unconditionally and be perpetually available. They must nurture and discipline, protect and stimulate, hold close and let go. They must make countless minute-by-minute decisions and plans for the distant future. Being a parent is more than should be asked of any human being, and the least that must be asked, must be required. In theory, I know all this to be absolutely true, and I have no difficulty understanding its intricacies. But personally I have never experienced it, *either as a child or as a parent. Desperately as I wanted to be that sort of father, I was not. I passed it on to my daughter Emily. She excels at it. Until now, she has been the consummate mother. Especially with this last child, it is more than should ever be asked of her, and yet it is vital for her children, for her, for our family, for the human race.*

Of Alexandra, for her first eighteen years, I expected a great deal, and I had every right and reason to do so. To her I gave everything I had not specifically assigned to the others, for her nature was simultaneously the most receptive and the most individuated, so that she could take what I gave to her and make it her own, imbue it with her own energy, release it into the world through her own sensibilities as well as mine. Her potential power was enormous.

But it was never realized. She wasted it. My greatest legacy was wilfully aborted. This child with the ability to take what I had to give and create of it a great gift to the world, this child who could have been the Kove family scion and standard-bearer—who alone could have justified not only her life but mine—said no. And left me.

Now once again she is here. I believe she is here. I cannot be sure of something I have longed for and forcibly put out of my consciousness for so long, but I believe she is here.

Eva Marie stirs. I move closer to her on the bed then lie down with her. I have lain with no one, certainly not with her, for a very long time. Her proximity awes and appals me.

I am awed and appalled by how utterly unreachable she is.

Alexandra. Alexandra, you and I both know what must be done here, and that you must do it for us all.

Bella is still nested on the floor, vocalizing only the occasional squeak and snuffle. I vowed to finish the first chapter of my father's *Handbook* in one sitting, a real stretch even though it's not very long. The instant I've read the last word of the last sentence, I scramble out of the chair, released, unsteady on my feet and desperate to *move*, to clear my mind or at least to think about something other than what I've just read. I pick up Bella. She starts, weakly flails. I hold her to me and begin to walk, crooning, as if she's the one I'm trying to calm.

Chapter 1 was less a bona fide history than a family tree. Relying more on lists of dates than on narrative, it related in broad, simplistic strokes the oft-told, skeletal tales—sketches, really; synopses— of our Slovak ancestors, my grandfather's birth and emigration, his marriage to my grandmother, the births of their three children of whom my father, Alexander—the grandfather of this infant in my arms—was the youngest, their deaths when he was seven years old.

There was one terse new anecdote. Because I've never heard it before, it quivers with significance, probably more than it really has. Out of the hall closet I grab one of Daddy's jackets. The sleeves are too short for me, and the shoulders tight. It carries an odour distinctly his; I've never before thought of him as having an odour, given how fastidious he's always been. Able to partially wrap Bella in it, I step out into the yellow night.

Against my will, I'm still mulling over the bit of narrative. I keep having the feeling I'm onto something, but I have no idea what.

Daddy's grandmother, Bella's great-great grandmother and my great-grandmother whom I never knew and therefore have no name for other than the given name Anna, which I cannot help pronouncing with an American accent, gave my grandfather a gift to take with him into the New World. Packaged and discrete as an heirloom, consciously given and received, the gift was the courage to break her heart by leaving the big sheltering stone house when they both knew he would never come back. She held him by the shoulders to bestow her blessing on him: "Go, son. I would go with you if I could. God help me, I would go instead of you. But I'm too afraid." She shook him. She kissed him. "Go. Be brave for us both."

"I'm not brave," he told her. "I'm afraid."

"It isn't bravery if you're not afraid." Like his mother's name, this adage must have sounded quite different in the language of my grandfather's youth, which he made a point not to pass down.

That's it. That's the whole story. What am I to make of that? It's in a book called *Handbook*, dedicated to me; obviously I'm supposed to make *something* of it. Something about gifts and curses, no doubt. Something about being sent off with the flag of the family waving in my hand. Something about carrying on my father's legacy—about *being* my father's legacy.

I'm repulsed by this whole thing. I'm repulsed by how profoundly it all attracts me. Shaky, light-headed, a little nauseated, I need desperately to talk to Martin and can't bring myself to call him.

Fuck it. I don't choose to accept the mission. Forget it, Daddy. I quit. Again.

But I'm outside no more than a matter of minutes; my foray into the dark yellow wood is no more than fifteen steps out and back. Then I'm striding into the house, tearing off my father's jacket, rushing to settle myself into his chair again and arrange the manuscript box on my lap. This time I keep Bella close to me, her head tucked under my chin and her feet pillowed in my abdomen, where I can feel her heartbeat without thinking about it.

Perhaps my mind has been elsewhere. Perhaps I have dozed off. I am now aware of a tremulous caress along my cheek and neck, stroking, an intensely familiar touch

I have not felt for many years. I draw back and murmur, "Herpie, stop it." But it is Eva Marie's hand, her thickened and stiffened fingers with the lovely mother-of-pearl nails grazing my skin in circles, loops, patters like rain, tiny tugs and taps. "Eva Marie, stop it."

She stops at once, and at once I wish she had not. "I'm sorry. You used to like it when I did that."

"I have never liked that," I lie to her. "You are obviously thinking of another man." She stiffens and pulls away, which I suspect was my goal. She is a dying woman, but she is also the woman who left me, left our children, and each overlays the other.

CHAPTER 2: HISTORY OF THE ALEXANDER KOVE FAMILY.

That's all it takes to seriously piss me off. Self-aggrandizing as a politician naming buildings after himself, my father claims—in writing, no less, obviously intended for posterity—way more credit than he has coming. What about "the Eva Marie Kove Family"? And I have spent what feels like a lifetime developing ways of defining myself other than as a member of any version of the Kove family. The temptation is strong to stop reading now, to blockade all points of entry against this skewed information and however it's intended to mess with my mind.

I don't, of course. I sit right there with the baby against my chest and my feet up in my father's recliner, in the conical yellow illumination his tall brass floor lamp sends over my right shoulder, and I know I'll read this thing from beginning to end, every damn word.

A few pages longer than Chapter 1, Chapter 2 has a bit more narrative. But the bulk of it, too, is just lists of names and dates, with a few annotations.

It begins with a notation of my parents' marriage. I'm shocked to realize I've never known the date, presumably because there were no wedding anniversaries to notice when I was growing up. Thinking of the sweet celebrations Martin and I have every year, I'm awash with homesickness, but it's no match for my father's *Handbook* and doesn't last long.

Grimly I note that Eva Marie Shivrinsky is presented as coming out of nowhere, as if she had no ancestry, no family tree. Her first appearance in this chronicle is when, via holy matrimony, she became part of the Alexander Kove Family.

The progeny of this union are duly listed. There I am, fourth of the five. Each of Alexander and Eva Marie's children is then allocated a separate page, on which are recorded marriage dates and the names and birth dates of their spouses and children. On my page, which I resent feeling compelled to look at, the date of my marriage to Martin is correct. Since none of my family was informed of the wedding, much less invited, this makes me uneasy. Ramon and Tara are listed, but with nasty little brackets around their names. How would Daddy have known their birth and adoption dates?

I check all my siblings' pages and note that the statistics are up to date. Galen's marriage to Vivian is there, and Bella's birth has been duly noted on Emily's page, which still has room for more. "There you are," I murmur to the baby. "Right there, see?"

Each of us then has another page. Under our names, which serve as headings, are listed words or phrases. Each of my siblings has only one:

GALEN:
SOCIAL/POLITICAL ACTIVISM

WILL:
GARDENING

VAUGHN:
MUSIC (COMPOSING AND PLAYING)

EMILY:
CHILD-BEARING AND -RAISING

I have a whole shitload. Lucky me.

ALEXANDRA:
TOLERANCE, ACCEPTANCE OF OTHERS,
EMOTIONAL RISK-TAKING, EXPANSIVE
AND PASSIONATE LOVE, MAINTENANCE
OF CONNECTIONS WITH OTHERS,
BEARING WITNESS TO OTHERS' PAIN,
HELPING E.M. IN LAST PHASE OF LIFE

The last phrase has to have been added very recently, though it's in the same script and the same ink as all the others.

He's made a long, looping bracket in the right-hand margin, encompassing all these items, and written in block letters on a diagonal beside the bracket a heading, as if he didn't know what to call this category of things until he'd listed them out. LOVE, it says.

Separate in its own category, outside the "love" bracket, is:

ALEXANDRA:
WRITING

"We had a good life together, didn't we, Alex?"

How can she ask this question? For a moment, I am profoundly confused. Is this not the woman who left that life? Can it be that my memory is false, that this narrative, which has seemed so real and true, is instead fictional and of my own creation?

My first reaction was to sneer, "Evidently not," and I do, but I add an attempt to verify what I thought I remembered: "You left our life together."

"Yes," she says, to my great relief and then cold fury. "But that doesn't mean it wasn't a good life."

"It put the lie to it. And your return now has put the lie to everything else."

"I don't know what that means."

"I failed you, Eva Marie." An admission of guilt is not an apology, but it is the most I will do.

"It wasn't you. It was me. I was weak. I felt like I was going to die or go crazy, hurt myself, hurt the kids. It was a terrible thing to do and I've never forgiven myself, but I still think it was the only thing I could do."

"I could have stopped you."

"No, Alex, you couldn't have. You didn't have that much control. You had a lot, but not that much."

"I could have made you happy. I simply was not sufficiently strong or patient or attentive."

She turns to me. I hear her, see her, smell her, feel the movement and the change in body heat. She takes my old face in her old hands and kisses me, and the taste of her is entirely unexpected. "Make me happy now," she whispers, and there is no doubt about what she means. I fear I will not be able to do it, but in this case there is, indisputably, no one to be my proxy. I lay my mouth against hers.

Bella stiffens and flings herself backward out of my lap, her body making muffled thuds against my knee, against the hard arm of the chair, onto the floor.

Chapter 13

She's not hurt. I tell myself she's not hurt, though I don't know how I'd know. She doesn't cry. There's no blood. She doesn't seem to have been at all affected by the fall. I have been, though; adrenaline makes my ears ring, my heart race, my hands tingle.

Rather than take that particular risk again, I make her comfortable on the floor—that is, I position her in a way that I would find comfortable, that most babies would find comfortable. Of course it's impossible to guess whether she does or if comfort has any meaning to her at all.

The next section of the handbook consists of a chapter for each of us in the form of experimental design and lab notes. Daddy's documentation appears meticulous, though admittedly I wouldn't know if he'd falsified or left things out. As always, he creates reality. As always, whenever I'm in any sort of contact with him, his reality—whether I buy into it or not, whether I accept it without realizing what I'm doing or reject it out of hand or try to sort out which parts of his world view make sense and which are utter bullshit—informs my own reality.

From Galen to Emily, his self-discipline as a change agent and resulting self-improvement, recorded in his tight script, are impressive. His learning curve is plotted by means of line graphs, specific interventions across the horizontal axes, incidence of desired behaviours along the vertical. My skin begins to crawl.

The chapter for Galen, the firstborn, records numerous false starts, unproven or disproved hypotheses, unforeseen results, flat-out errors. In the beginning, his efforts, though perhaps more organized and self-conscious than most, weren't really much out of the ordinary; certainly nothing here would require a magical or otherwise supernatural explanation. All parents make mistakes, often out of naiveté and an anxious hubris about how much influence they have—or ought to have—over their children. The desire to leave a legacy, to ensure that the next generation will be, by your definition, better than yours—healthier, wealthier, better educated, saner—might even be an instinct in the service of the evolution of the species. But there's something more than a little creepy about how our father went about it, and about the very fact that he wrote it down in such detail, accurate and complete or not.

My mind fuzzes, doing its best not to take anything from him. From nearly a lifetime of practise, the technique is highly developed, but this time it's overridden by a need both more primal and more immediate. I read.

> GALEN:
> AGE 28-33 MONTHS. READ BOOKS
> AND WATCHED MOVIES RE: SLAVERY,
> HOLOCAUST. FOCUS ON GRAPHIC
> VIOLENCE, HORROR, TO MAKE IMPRES-
> SION ON UNDEVELOPED CONSCIENCE.
> DISCUSSED WITH CHILD IN 5-MINUTE
> INCREMENTS TO ACCOMMODATE AT-
> TENTION SPAN.
>
> HYPOTHESIS: INCIDENCE OF EXPRES-
> SIONS OF OUTRAGE AND SYMPATHY
> RE: SOCIAL INJUSTICE WILL INCREASE.
>
> RESULT: NO MEASURABLE OR OB-
> SERVABLE EFFECT. CHILD AWAKENED
> SCREAMING 11 TIMES: NIGHTMARES?
>
> AGE 36 MONTHS. CRIPPLED CHILD
> SOLE GUEST INVITED TO G'S BIRTHDAY
> PARTY.

HYPOTHESIS: PERSONAL EXPOSURE TO LESS FORTUNATE WILL RESULT IN INCREASED TOLERANCE.

RESULT: CRIPPLED CHILD DESTROYED G'S PRESENTS. INCREASED FREQUENCY AND SEVERITY OF EXPRESSED HOSTILITY BY G TOWARD DIVERSE POPULATIONS.

AGE 36-44 MONTHS. TOOK G TO POLITICAL RALLIES FOR DEMOCRATIC CONGRESSIONAL CANDIDATE. SUPPRESSED OWN DISTASTE FOR MOB MENTALITY TO EMPHASIZE PARTY ATMOSPHERE, "FUN," IDEALISM.

HYPOTHESIS: CHILD WILL DEMONSTRATE ENJOYMENT, EXCITEMENT, DESIRE TO PARTICIPATE IN MORE SUCH ACTIVITIES.

RESULT: CHILD WHINED TO GO HOME THEN FELL ASLEEP.

AGE 47 MONTHS. SHOT RABBIT IN FRONT OF CHILD.

Jesus. I look away from the handbook, take a few deep breaths, read the stark line again.

> AGE 47 MONTHS. SHOT RABBIT IN FRONT OF CHILD. DISCUSSED ANIMALS' RIGHT TO LIVE.

> HYPOTHESIS: DRAMA WILL BE SUFFICIENT TO INSTIL CONCERN FOR ANIMAL RIGHTS. RESULT: CHILD INITIATED DISCUSSION OF INCIDENT SIX TIMES IN SUBSEQUENT WEEK.

This went on for pages, for years of Galen's life. More than once, Daddy's efforts to instil in his first child a sensitivity to social injustice, together with the knowledge of how to work for social change bordered on abusive; he placed my brother in situations deliberately designed to be emotionally disturbing and sometimes even put him in harm's way. Some of it worked, but apparently not well enough to suit him. So then he took a more direct approach.

Between Eva Marie and myself there never was much eroticism. In point of fact, I have long suspected this form of arousal to be primarily delusion. Having of course read Freud, I acknowledge the possibility that I have sublimated erotic passion into more useful pursuits, such as bettering the human condition. Would that more people saw fit to do the same.

At any rate, the prolonged contact of my mouth with Eva Marie's, though admittedly rather tender, is not a kiss in any usual sense of the word. It is an attempt, however doomed, to establish a usable link between us where there is none. When her coughing causes both of us to turn our heads in self-protection, nothing but bodily fluid has passed between us, and little enough of that.

"Oh, Alex," she murmurs. "Don't you want to know what I've been doing all these years? Aren't you the least bit curious?"

For a long time after she left, I was desperate to know and not to know what she was doing and with whom. Then I stopped thinking about it, stopped directly thinking about her altogether, a difficult discipline but useful and necessary. Now she is not someone I know or care to know in any personal way. Intimate knowledge of another person costs dearly; I have long ago exhausted my available resources. This is Alexandra's responsibility.

Straining to sit up, I mimic her tone and phrasing. "Not the least bit."

Her tears do not move me. Her wheezing and rattling respiration does not move me. I will not be moved. For reasons I cannot fathom, she persists. "I married again."

This ought not to come as a surprise. I ought not to respond at all. "There is no divorce."

"I've never told him I was married before. I've never told him about you or the kids. We never wanted children."

"My, my, a double life." Despite myself, despite my icy fury and revulsion, I am intrigued and even a bit admiring.

She stirs, precipitating a protracted coughing fit. I do wish she had the sense to stay still. "No, not double. I left this life, Alex. I never looked back."

"Untrue." I stab my finger in her direction, though the room is dark and I doubt she can see me even if she should happen to be looking right at me. "Untrue! As evidenced by the fact that you are here now, demanding something. Demanding a great deal, as a matter of fact. An outrageous demand. Why are you here? Has your—husband—" I can scarcely say the word— "your husband died or left you? How unfortunate for you. How ironic."

"No, no, we'll celebrate our thirty-eighth anniversary on New Year's Eve. I'm determined to live that long. He's a good man, Alex. We've been happy."

"How nice." Numerous useless queries clutter my mind: Are you saying your death is imminent? How have you explained your current absence to this "husband" with whom you have been so "happy"? How did you get here? Where did you come from? What is your husband's name? How dare you? There is no point in uttering any of them.

"But you," she says, and I hear her turn toward me, "Alex, you're the one I need now. Not so much you personally—no offence—but that thing you do, the way you just insert into people some attribute or skill, like Vaughn's music or Alexandra's writing."

"This is nonsense," I manage to say. "This is pure fantasy."

She doesn't even hesitate. "Don't, Alex. I don't have time for this. Maybe you didn't realize I knew what you were doing, but you know very well what I'm talking about. Since I've been here I've watched you still doing it. I need not to be afraid. My husband is more afraid of my death than I am. He can't give me peace. But you can. You can just put it into me. Please, Alex."

WILL:
AGE 8 MONTHS 8 DAYS. IN GARDEN
WITH ME 2.5 HOURS.

HYPOTHESIS: EXPOSURE TO GARDEN
IN PRESENCE OF TRUSTED ADULT WILL
INCREASE FAMILIARITY AND PLEA-
SURE.

RESULT: BY EVENING, INFANT FEVER-
ISH, VOMITING. TAKEN BY MOTHER TO
E.R.

DX: HEAT EXHAUSTION.

AGE 17 MONTHS. OBSERVED HOLD-
ING PETUNIA CAREFULLY, SMELLING,

TOUCHING TONGUE TO PETALS. VER-
BALIZATION OF PLEASURE.

EXTRAPOLATION: CHILD POSSESSES
INHERENT APPRECIATION OF FLORA.

HYPOTHESIS: CHILD POSSESSES IN-
HERENT APTITUDE FOR GARDENING.
GAVE CHILD HIS OWN POT OF PETU-
NIAS TO TEND WITH MY ASSISTANCE.

HYPOTHESIS: EXPRESSIONS OF APPRE-
CIATION WILL INCREASE IN FREQUENCY
AND INTELLIGIBILITY.

RESULT: PLANTS DEAD, CHILD DIS-
TRAUGHT.

AGE 22 MONTHS. APPARENT EX-
TREME REVULSION RE: TOMATO
WORM. SCREAMING. NIGHTMARES.
REFUSES TO EAT TOMATOES EVEN
WHEN ALL OTHER FOOD WITHHELD.

It's hard for me to take this gardening thing seriously. Talk about your ridiculous control battles.
Skimming, I laugh aloud at the foolishness of it,
but I'm also horrified. Again, our father's determination that his child will do what he himself was

unable or unwilling to do came perilously close to child abuse. Heat exhaustion? Withholding food? When Will was five years old the entries stopped, and I can guess where they will pick up in the next chapter.

VAUGHN:

AGE 17-57 MONTHS. TANTRUMS, AVERAGE FREQUENCY 2/DAY, AVERAGE DURATION 62 MINUTES. BANGING HEAD, SCRATCHING SELF, SHRIEKING. APPARENTLY SOOTHED BY DVORAK'S "GRAND CANYON." SUBSEQUENT TANTRUMS DELIBERATELY PRECIPITATED BY PHYSICAL RESTRAINT AND REMOVAL OF DESIRED OBJECTS. OBSERVED DECREASE IN TANTRUM SEVERITY AND DURATION (SEE GRAPH):

LENA HORNE, "STORMY WEATHER" AND "MISTY": 22 AND 21 MIN

APPALACHIAN FOLK MUSIC, "BARBARA ALLEN": 43 MIN

IRISH BALLAD, "DANNY BOY": 31 MIN

JOHN PHILIP SOUSA, VARIOUS MARCHES: 41 MIN

SIBELIUS, "FINLANDIA": 16 MIN

GERSHWIN, "RHAPSODY IN BLUE": 19 MIN

MOZART, "DON GIOVANNI": 23 MIN

EXTRAPOLATION: CHILD POSSESSES INHERENT APPRECIATION FOR MUSIC OF MANY TYPES.

HYPOTHESIS: CHILD POSSESSES APTITUDE FOR CREATING MUSIC VIA PLAYING INSTRUMENTS AND COMPOSITION.

AGE 48 MONTHS. CHILD GIVEN DRUMS AND WOODEN FLUTE FOR BIRTHDAY. BEGAN PLAYING IMMEDIATELY. WITHIN 24 HOURS, COMPOSING.

Daddy seems to have been right about this one. From an early age Vaughn apparently responded positively to music, as if his appreciation and talent for it might indeed have been innate. Determinedly sceptical, I re-read the notes looking for indications that Daddy imposed his will on Vaughn no matter what the cost, as with my two oldest brothers, but from the notes it seems pretty clear that in this case he had only to nurture what was already there.

Considering what I understand the next phase of the project to have been, I'm thinking Vaughn may not have sections in subsequent chapters at all, that our father may have been done with him. I'm sad for him, which is not the reaction I'd have expected.

"I am retired," I insist to Eva Marie. She laughs. "I am not joking. I am no longer engaged in active—" Having never spoken of this aloud or thought about it in terms of label or category, I do not know what term to use.

Almost shyly, but with an offensive proprietary smugness, she offers, "I've always sort of enjoyed thinking I was once married to a wizard."

"We are still married." The correction is reflexive and off the point, but I let it stand.

"And are you a wizard, Alex?"

" 'Wizard' is a silly term," I retort before I fully realize, with disgust, that she is being coy, even flirtatious.

I am also, quite unexpectedly, what I can only call desperate for her, for Eva Marie, my wife, this woman whom I had thought would never again be any part of my life. I am desperate for contact. Because of that, I know myself to be in mortal danger, and I move as quickly as possible to escape it. She gets to her feet, not a single movement but a series of unbalanced fits and starts that cause her wholly inadequate breath to rattle in her thin chest. I cannot allow this or any other thing about her to impede me. The flat of my hand is on Vaughn's rough door when she cries, "Stop it, Alex! There's something! I know there's something!"

Wheezing and swaying, she leans against the board-and-cement-block shelves Vaughn uses as dresser, desk, bookcase, and medicine cabinet. The oxygen tank stands beside the bed, unattached to her. When she speaks again, she has lowered her voice, but it shakes.

"You have some kind of power. You do something magical or at least unnatural, I know you do. It's like telepathy, or telekinesis, or voodoo. You cast a spell or you replace who a person is with who you want them to be. I watched you do it with all our kids. I felt you doing it with me. I felt you inside me, in my mind. That's why I had to get away. And it's why I've come back now. Please, Alex, I know you do!"

The extended outburst has taken nearly all her breath and strength. Coughing, she totters toward me. I remove my hand from the door, turn, reach to fend her off.

The two of us meet somewhere in the space that was between us. Wrapped in each other's frail arms, supporting each other and pulling each other down, we sink carefully but nonetheless precipitously to the dusty wooden floor.

The "Alexandra" section of the Experimental Design chapter is long. As I mark the beginning of it with one hand and flip through it to mark the end with the other, then gather the pages between thumb and forefinger to turn all at once, I can't help noting numerous lists and graphs interspersing single-spaced narratives with hardly any paragraphs. I also can't help noting the page count: sixty-four pages, just for me. Just for the first eighteen years of my life.

The tightness in my throat has spread across my chest and back. Nervous energy races up and down my extremities like running lights. My hands and feet prickle. I'd think I was having a coronary if there weren't plenty of reason for an anxiety attack. I almost wish I were having a heart attack instead.

Balancing the manuscript box on one hand and squeezing the "Alexandra" chapter between the other forefinger and thumb, I stumble into my room. It takes a while but I finally find an alligator clip big enough to hold sixty-four pages. Feeling a little safer, I can go back to Daddy's chair to resume reading.

EMILY:
AGE 11 MONTHS. PLACED CHILD'S
FINGER ON INJURED BIRD IN SHOE-
BOX. MOTHER COMPLAINED OF POSSI-
BLE DISEASE.

HYPOTHESIS: CHILD WILL DEMON-
STRATE THE BEGINNINGS OF COMPAS-
SION.

RESULT: NO IDENTIFIABLE REACTION.

AGE 19 MONTHS. OBSERVED COMFORTING UNJUSTLY PUNISHED SIBLING.

HYPOTHESIS: BEHAVIOUR REPRESENTS COMPASSION. REPLICATED CONDITIONS BY UNJUSTLY PUNISHING SAME AND OTHER SIBLINGS.

RESULTS: NO OBSERVABLE RESPONSE FROM CHILD.

AGE 23 MONTHS. HERPIE ASSIGNED TO SIMULATE INJURY.

OBSERVATIONS: CHILD ATTEMPTED TO KILL H BY JUMPING ON HER. H SLIGHTLY INJURED.

AGE 29 MONTHS. CHILD OBSERVED COMFORTING TEARFUL MOTHER.

UNABLE TO REPLICATE.

AGE 36-42 MONTHS. CHILD GIVEN LIFELIKE BABY DOLL AS ONLY BIRTHDAY PRESENT. AFTER INITIAL REACTION, APPEARS DISINTERESTED.

ORDERED HER TO PLAY WITH DOLL
MINIMUM TWO 30-MINUTE SESSIONS
PER DAY.

HYPOTHESIS: NURTURING ABILITY
CAN BE TAUGHT. NURTURING BE-
HAVIOURS WILL INCREASE.

RESULT: NURTURING BEHAVIOURS
INCREASE IN FREQUENCY AND DURA-
TION (SEE GRAPH) DESPITE CHILD'S
CONTINUING PROTESTS.

This was evidently the turning point for my sister, when our father's will won out over hers. The central theme of her life can be seen as having developed from there. By the age of twelve she was babysitting several times a week. All through high school she was a camp counsellor, day care aide, candy striper on the children's ward, assistant Brownie leader. When she was barely eighteen she married Earl and they had their first child before her nineteenth birthday.

Seeing documentation of the "before" and "after" is chilling. I'm also aware of what can only be called a thrill.

Okay, it's time. No more putting it off. Fish or cut bait. I'm having trouble getting air into my lungs and my head is spinning, but it's time. Shit or get off the pot.

I take the paper clip off the grouped pages, turn to the beginning of the "Alexandra" Experimental Design chapter, and read.

"I must study. I must research and experiment. I do not know the formula for what you want."

"I don't have time for all that."

"This is for Alexandra to do."

"I don't have time, Alex. I have to get home."

"Home?"

"You didn't think I came here to die, did you?"

"Of course not."

"I came here to learn how to die. Then I'm going home."

"So, if I understand correctly, I am being asked to give this to you, at considerable cost to myself, and then to send you on your way back to your husband."

She has the decency to hesitate before she replies, "That's right."

ALEXANDRA:
GESTATION AGE: 20 WEEKS.

It takes a moment for me to realize what this means. With me he started *in utero*. Even inside my mother I wasn't safe from him. Even when I was still physically connected to her, receiving everything one would have thought I needed directly from her, he was reaching in, inside her body and inside my still-forming brain, to curse and bless me with his gift.

Gifts, plural. Unlike my brothers and sister, I wasn't given a unidirectional, single, discrete assignment. He gave me all sorts of shit. He gave me things he'd given them—Galen's social activism, Emily's compulsion to love—but in more expansive form, as if not trusting what he'd done with them or having decided he could raise the stakes.

This might make some crazy sort of sense if I'd been the last child born after my siblings were old enough for our father to observe what he had or had not wrought with them. Given my birth order, though, and the closeness of all of our ages, it really looks as if he singled me out from the beginning—from before the beginning, depending on your point of view.

ALEXANDRA:
GESTATION AGE: 20 WEEKS.

HYPOTHESIS: PASSION FOR READING AND WRITING CAN BE INSTILLED VERY EARLY. INSTRUCTED MOTHER RE: READING TO FOETUS 2X DAY. MOTHER AGREED BUT DID NOT FOLLOW THROUGH.

GESTATION AGE: 24-37 WEEKS.

HYPOTHESIS: SEE ABOVE. READ PO-
ETRY ALOUD (WHISPER, MOUTH TO
MOTHER'S ABDOMEN) 15 MIN/NIGHT
AFTER MOTHER ASLEEP.

RESULTS: FOETAL MOVEMENT AP-
PEARED TO INCREASE WITH READING,
BUT NOT STATISTICALLY SIGNIFICANT.

LABOUR AND DELIVERY.

HYPOTHESIS: SEE ABOVE. RECITED
"THE PASSIONATE SHEPHERD TO HIS
LOVE." MOTHER AND HOSPITAL PER-
SONNEL EXPRESSED ANNOYANCE.

RESULTS: NO OBSERVABLE REACTION
FROM INFANT.

The image of my father—by no means oblivious
to other people's feelings but utterly dismissive of
them—declaiming sappy poetry while my mother
was in the throes of labour and I struggled both to
enter the world and to stay in the womb, is such vin-
tage Alexander Kove that I guffaw and shudder at
the same time.

AGE 0-12 MONTHS.

HYPOTHESIS: SEE ABOVE. READ TO
CHILD 1 HR/DAY. CONTENT LESS IM-
PORTANT THAN INSTILLING LOVE OF
WORDS.

RESULTS: INFANT DEMONSTRATES
PLEASURE: CALMS WHEN AGITATED,
SMILES, COOS. (SEE GRAPH.)

I swear I remember this. The feel of my father's body as I lay on his chest. The sound of his voice and his heartbeat. The smell of him, different when he read to me than any other time. I hadn't remembered it until now, and of course it's not likely that I really remember it now, but I swear I do.

Daddy read to me throughout my childhood, long after he'd stopped with my siblings, because I responded. My section of the handbook is festooned with charts and graphs showing how I responded, and I do remember that, clearly.

When I was thirty months old, he began having me memorize Dickinson poems, on the theory, I suppose, that if a toddler could memorize "Twinkle, Twinkle, Little Star" she could memorize "A Narrow Fellow in the Grass." Which I could. By the age of four and a half, I was reading to him. I remember that.

I wrote my first book when I was not quite five, for my mother for Mother's Day. Daddy helped me.

It was a story about an adorable anthropomorphic snake who follows a little girl to school and wins over her classmates and her teacher. It had maybe six pages and a cardboard cover, and was bound with red yarn stuck through inexpertly punched holes and tied in a bow. He insisted I illustrate the cover with a smiling snake, and my heart sank and leaped and sank again at the way his interest in me intensified when he saw the drawing, for I knew he was thinking I had artistic talent. Newly remembering this, I wonder why he never added that to his experimental design, and I feel both spared and shunned. These mixed emotions are getting really old.

At about that same time, he began introducing other things. Other "mental substances."

AGE 3 YEARS 2 MONTHS.

INTRODUCED CHILD TO ORGANI-
ZATION SUPPORTING CHILDREN IN
THIRD WORLD COUNTRIES. POSTED
PHOTO IN HER ROOM, TOLD HER
STORIES OF HUNGER AND NO TOYS.
ASSIGNED CHORES FOR WHICH SHE
EARNS MONEY TO SEND.

HYPOTHESIS: CHILD WILL ACHIEVE
BEGINNING UNDERSTANDING OF RE-
SPONSIBILITY TO OTHERS.

RESULTS: CHILD CRIED OVER PHOTO
AND STORIES OF NEEDY CHILD, CRIED
OVER BEING REQUIRED TO GIVE UP
MONEY.

I had forgotten about that picture, all in shades of grainy grey, that he taped to the corner of the mirror on my closet door sternly at a three-year-old's eye level. I had forgotten about the big dark eyes that followed me around my room, into my dreams, into my conscience and my view of the world. I had forgotten about the shiny quarters he paid me for picking up sticks in the yard, putting my baby sister's toys into the toy box, dusting the bookshelves in the living room—stacks of shiny quarters he dropped one-by-one, for maximum effect, into my cupped hands and then made me give back to him, one-by-one, to send to the girl with the big dark eyes. I had forgotten his pride in my sacrifice, and his disappointment with my attitude about it. It all comes back to me now, and I want to tell him he was wrong, he misjudged me even then. I did get the point, and the point has stayed with me my whole life. And, though still grudgingly, I'm grateful.

AGE 4 YEARS 2 MONTHS-5 YEARS 6
MONTHS.

ASSIGNED A TO DICTATE 1 LETTER/
WEEK TO SPONSORED CHILD, INCLUD-
ING DRAWINGS, STORIES, POEMS,
SIGNATURE.

I think: You clever bastard. Here's where the incul-
cation of writing as a holy art form began, neatly
tied to moral responsibility for a little extra punch.

AGE 6 YEARS.

ASSIGNED A TO WRITE POEMS FOR
PEOPLE SHE LOVES AS HER BIRTHDAY
GIFTS TO THEM.

He means that he made me write poems on *my*
birthday as *my* gifts to *other* people. It's a lovely, generous idea, though a bit much for a six-year-old. I've
done it every year since I can remember, and until
now had thought it my own invention. Martin keeps
all the poems I've written for him in a blue binder,
and I've seen how he lays his palms on it. *Martin.* I'm
weak with missing Martin.

I think: You did have a thing about your children's
birthdays as teachable moments, didn't you? And I
wonder: For my sixth birthday, did I write a poem for
him? I hope so. God, I hope so.

My section of the handbook goes on like this for many entries over many pages, and I read every word. As my recorded age increases I remember more and more of the incidents: poetry contests, pen pals (at one point in junior high, eleven of them in eight different poor countries), field trips with Daddy and then alone to soup kitchens and cancer wards in order to write about them, volunteering after school in a nursing home to write oral histories, trying and failing to organize anti-war rallies at the high school.

Reading and remembering all this takes a long time. Bella doesn't interrupt or distract me, but it's not as if I forget she's here.

Chapter 14

The handbook has been carefully constructed so as to appear exhaustive, but that's an illusion, a calculated ruse. A lie.

It does not account for the sense I've had all my life that my father continually reached inside my mind and—literally, palpably—altered it to suit his purposes. That at my core I was—am—his deliberate creation. That there's nothing about me that didn't come straight from him. That without him I am, have always been, will be nothing.

It does not account for the lifelong sensation that has variously taken the form of drowning, of kinesthetic disorientation, of deliciously and dangerously wavering boundaries between me and not-me. Of simultaneously dissolving and being granted form.

I haven't come this far to stop now.

In a fury that feels both unprecedented and familiar, I leap out of my father's chair, fling his handbook behind me onto the seat, and set about ransacking the house. Bella stays on the living room floor, quiet.

First I search his room. High this time on what has morphed into an extreme, intimate violation of his privacy, I strip his bed, rifle through his drawers, plunder his closet, pull books off shelves, empty bags and boxes onto the floor. Some of these things are my mother's, hoarded all these years, affording me now the fantasy—doubly horrible, doubly satisfying—of violating her, too, coming close to her, too. I rummage through socks, underwear, tax records, old greeting cards, dime store jewellery, medications, opened and unopened mail.

Not finding what I'm looking for, I storm out of the dishevelled room, make a quick detour to check on Bella, and start on the kitchen. By the time pans, utensils, dishes, paper goods, boxes and cans of food, the contents of the refrigerator are piled on the counters and the floor, Bella is screaming, maybe from the noise, maybe not. I go to her, sit on the floor and hold her until she calms; there's no reason to think my presence or absence makes any difference to her, and holding her doesn't calm me, either, but I don't know what else to do.

The rush from searching and destroying propels me into the bathroom. I pull unfolded towels out of the linen closet, dump shampoo and soap into the small pool where the shower still doesn't quite drain, empty the cabinet under the sink of toilet paper and a half-full trash can and wads of tissue that didn't make it into the trash. The meagre contents of the medicine cabinet, jumbled onto the sink, aren't nearly as revealing as one might think.

The living room is quieter and takes longer. I try to be careful not to disturb Bella, but she doesn't react anyway. Pillows off the couch, magazines out of numerous racks, books off floor-to-ceiling shelves, furniture away from walls and some lighter pieces overturned. Nothing. I'm panting and flushed, have no clear idea what all this is about, but know that I have found nothing.

Searching the other bedrooms, empty since my siblings moved out, takes little time and discharges little of my mounting frenzy. Searching my room takes longer because, oddly, it seems imperative to hunt through my own things as well as the stuff that doesn't belong to me. Nothing.

Without conscious decision then, I'm sliding the baby into the carrier and slinging it onto my back. She startles, gasps, waves arms and legs, but none of that has any effect. I'm out into the dawning woods, charging through lemon-coloured sunrise toward my father's cave.

The woods are familiar and at the same time strange, familiarity and strangeness each intensifying the other. There's been no kinesthetic or psychological disorientation this time. No need for Herpie as narrow guide, or for Daddy to tell me what to do. I have no trouble finding my way, even with the distraction of the baby on my back, so still and light I keep having to reach awkwardly behind me to assure myself she's there. There's no guarantee she'd have any discernible reaction if she slipped out or was carried off. I don't know that I could give anybody else directions to where we're going—explain to Bella, for instance—but I seem to know.

The rock overhang is exactly where I expected it to be, and I go right to it, as if there were a road. It doesn't take long, either. When I get there, the light in the woods is still pale mottled lemon, shimmering on dewy leaves, sparkling here and there on boulder and pebble like Hansel and Gretel's crumbs.

Not even out of breath, I carefully shrug the baby carrier off my shoulders. Bella hardly moves as I lift her out, except for her tiny breathing and tinier heartbeat. After some trial and error, which she doesn't protest or seem to notice, I find a way to hold her to my chest with one arm and get down onto my other hand and knees. *Martin,* I think once, and crawl in.

There's no passage into my father's hidden place, no transition from outside to inside. You're in it immediately. Deep enough in the woods and far enough inside rock that any effect of the rising sun—or rotating earth, depending on your point of view—has dissipated before

I've gone in a body length. The place is dusty and dank. I don't feel even the presence of dawn behind me, though I can still hear dawn birds, the dry three-part non-harmony of doves, a more liquid three-part song whose singer I wish I could name. "Listen," I whisper to the baby. "Hear that?"

Always orderly to a fault—though not all that clean, what with plant debris, spider webs, moulted snake skins, pollen, rock dust—the space I've come to think of as my father's laboratory feels intensely organized now, and I survey it in a much more organized way than I have before. About a quarter of it is neatly filled by containers of various sorts, on the floor, stacked on each other, on rudimentary board-and-rock shelves. My attention is caught by the fact that they're all labelled, but then I see that the labels are in some sort of code. Who did the old son-of-a-bitch think would ever be in here snooping?

The urge is strong to ransack the laboratory even worse than the house, to dump out the contents of all the fucking coded containers into one amalgamated mess that would eventually seep into the ground, to break things and destroy the order and just generally create havoc. I resist the temptation, deferring this particular gratification until I've either found whatever it is I'm looking for or determined beyond a shadow of a doubt that it's not here. Then, one way or the other, look out.

Ground-to-roof against the back wall are books. Some are on shelves, some stacked, some in boxes. I'd noticed the books before, of course; they'd be hard to miss. But now their cumulative presence looms.

There are also notebooks and boxes of index cards, pens and markers in a Big Gulp cup, three flashlights, a battery-operated camping lantern. In a suitcase—not in the least battered, though I'm sure it's ancient— he's stored pillows and pads, a lap robe I remember sending him one year for Christmas and am inordinately touched to see he's been using, a winter jacket, gloves, knit cap, rain poncho, old-fashioned galoshes, handheld fan. A plastic grocery bag holds several rolls of toilet paper; I don't even want to think about what that implies.

There's no chance of creating my own space here. I don't even want to. Intrusion is part of the point. I set about adapting his space for my use. Ambient light, produced by the lantern and two of the flashlights pointed so that their beams crisscross, stays in discrete rays, diffusing hardly at all in here. The other flashlight I use to scan the rest of the cave, its beam penetrating but in no way scattering or even muting the darkness, like an eye on a stem.

It takes no time at all to find what I've been looking for, and only a split second to realize that's what it is. A green spiral notebook on a flowered TV tray, it's labelled in black Magic Marker and not in code:

251

HANDBOOK II: DIRECT INFUSION. I'm aware that Bella's diaper is wet, but she can wait.

I'm not really surprised by what's recorded here, but I am incredulous. My father's got balls, I have to give him that. I can't believe it, and yet it's so in character. I was doing what he wanted. But it wasn't enough for him. Why am I not surprised.

It wasn't just me. Once again, he started with Galen and worked his way down in the intensified version of ordinary parenting he'd developed to such a high level. Not content with moulding us, he embarked upon a much more forthright, insidious, and effective approach. This is where things get really weird.

I carry the notebook into the pool of light from the lantern and flashlights, one of which is visibly dimming. The pillows don't know my body, of course; my father's body has made lumps and depressions, which are hideously uncomfortable for me. Settling Bella in my lap is a lot like arranging a stiff plastic doll. I train the remaining flashlight on the notebook, meticulously adjusting the beam before I dare open the cover.

Some of the spirals are bent. Stuck in them are fringed strips where pages were torn out. The green of the cover is mottled from long exposure. Or maybe it was always like that, came from the store like that. Or maybe the darker and lighter, rougher and smoother places result from a subtle interplay between what was already in the cardboard and what has been put into it by external forces. Or maybe I'm just making this up as I go along.

Doves coo, and that other silvery three-note song repeats and repeats. Bella coughs lightly but there seems to be nothing any more wrong with her than usual, so I just tuck the edge of her blue blanket a little differently around her ears. The cave smells like a place even more buried than it is. Already my back and knees hurt. I open the notebook and bend close over the baby to read, a position I won't be able to hold for long.

"Alex. Wait."

Past taking hold of the door handle, I have not moved to exit, though I intended to do so. Therefore, Eva Marie's exhortation is gratuitous, and the fact that I remain in place until she laboriously reaches me is as much my decision as hers.

Expecting her to collapse into me, I brace myself against the wall and ready my arms. But she very lightly takes my hands, one and then the other, labouring for breath and trembling but maintaining her own balance. "I don't know how it works, but I used to watch you do it. When you want somebody to be a certain way, you just make them be that way. It's like you inject them with a concentrate of whatever it is—Emily's motherliness,

Alexandra's writing—right into their brains or their hearts or their souls."

Long having found the concept of "soul" insipid, I snort.

"Or wherever it is. Do that for me. Inject me with peace about dying."

"You expect too much of me, Eva Marie. I myself have some trepidation about death," I admit baldly.

"You don't garden, either, or make music. Or write."

This last, of course, is not entirely accurate, but I see no point in disabusing her of her misapprehension.

"Give me this, Alex. You have it to give. Don't try to pretend you don't."

"Why would I—" But she does not stop there.

"And tell me what you're doing as you do it. I want to understand."

Acceptance of one's own mortality has long been yet another on my list of attributes essential to the improvement and advancement of the human race, and utterly beyond my capacity. Until now, I have had neither the opportunity nor the wherewithal to induce it in anyone else, either, and had all but reconciled myself to this fundamental flaw in my character and will. Now, suddenly, a possibility seems to have presented itself, and I must reconsider my position, an obligation exhausting and dangerous from which, of course, I will not turn away. I have always been called to perform difficult and thankless tasks, and I have never shirked my responsibility.

Dreading this most welcome opportunity, I concede, "I am willing to make an attempt."

"Thank you," she breathes.

Together we make our way to Vaughn's only two chairs, on either side of the east window. The pane is grimy, but it lets in a hint of sunrise; though light is unnecessary for the procedure, it illumines her nicely from behind and sparkles through the mist of her thin white hair. The chairs are dirty, worn, fuzzy with exposed stuffing, but might be sturdy and comfortable enough.

Standing unsteadily in front of her as she lowers herself into the grey chair, I formulate a hasty and not very reassuring plan as to what to do if she should fall. Among the few and unsatisfactory options, staying with her until Vaughn returns seems best. It has, in fact, a certain appeal.

However, she does not fall. When she is seated, she is shaking and pale, but I can see she is ready. Hands folded in her lap, legs crossed at the ankles; she smiles up at me in a shy and flirtatious manner I had not known I remembered.

Joints creaking, I sit in the brown chair, well away from her. It has been a long time since I have done this at all, and never by request of the intended recipient. I have also never performed for an audience, like a stage magician, nor did I ever anticipate circumstances under which I would consider such a thing.

I have also never documented the process aloud. Doing so will alter it. I cannot think where to start.

"Don't you have to touch me?"

"No."

"Oh. I thought you would have to touch me."

"No."

"Is it just words, then? Like a spell?"

"No. It comes out of silence." *After so long away from me, after all this time without her and all the harm she has done me and my children, who is she to ask for, even to know about, my single talent, the seed and fruit of who I am?*

She nods and shifts in her seat. "I'll be quiet then."

I want to talk to her. I want to leave her. I want her to die, here and now, frightened and untouched by me. I want to take her in my arms, die with her, open her up and pour into her everything I have and everything I can imagine in whatever time is left to us. I am not strong enough for this. I must be. Out of love for Eva Marie and devotion to the world, I must be strong enough. This has always been my way, my scourge and my salvation.

The deepening of ordinary quiet into and beyond still-ness requires considerably longer than it once did, and is far more painful. Eva Marie appears to be the one in a trance, while my restless mind continues to notice and internally comment upon the external environment: dust in the air of Vaughn's undusted house, pale gold light steadily brightening through the window un-curtained except by dirt and vine, Eva Marie's powdery rose perfume.

Reaching the place I need to reach is an act not of will but of surrender; I remember this in principle before I remember how to do it. Surrender has never come naturally to me, and now I am long out of practice. The difficulty of it, the pain it causes me, assures me of its value and truth.

Every time I have given to someone else—forced into someone else—an undeveloped part of myself, I personally have been diminished in order to enrich the world at large. Giving to Eva Marie the acceptance of death I have long seen on the horizon of my soul, as it were, but never been able to approach for myself, might well be my undoing. And the sacrifice is the meaning of my life.

PROTOCOL

1. SENDER FILLS CONSCIOUSNESS AND SENSORIUM WITH THAT WHICH REQUIRES INTERVENTION: PROBLEM TO BE SOLVED, VOID TO BE FILLED, SITUATION TO BE RECTIFIED, QUALITY OR CHARACTERISTIC TO BE IMPARTED (HEREINAFTER REFERRED TO AS "MENTAL SUBSTANCE").

When the intent was for Vaughn to create music, I had first to be filled with music and the need to create it. In order to infuse Will with the compulsion to garden, it was necessary to be infused myself with the sight, sound, smell, feel, taste of things grown in the garden, and with the compulsion to grow them. Parental devotion, social and political activism, adventurousness, determination to forge and maintain deep connections with other living things, creativity and talent—I was both able and required to achieve these states in what might be called my imagination though that term is pallid and hardly does it justice.

For the sake of accuracy, it must be acknowledged that this part of the procedure was by no means unpleasant. In point of fact, it was ecstatic. Dangerously so. The pain, the profound self-inflicted wound, came from extracting each fully felt passion out of my own heart and passing it into someone else's.

Now, death enters my awareness like a creature in a room. I will die. Everyone I know will die. Despite primal terror, I do not turn away.

"Talk to me, Alex. What are you doing?"

My voice catches in my throat. I cough, swallow, try again. "I am taking in death. I am taking in your death."

She cries out, "No!" but also does not flee, stays where she is, her body rigid in the chair, her mind still available to me.

"No!" I too cry out, perhaps aloud, and only by casting it as a gift to Eva Marie and to humanity am I able to keep my own mind available, my own body from collapsing under the weight, my own heart and brain from seizing up.

*I will die. Eva Marie will die. Everyone I know will die.
This most intimate of certainties fills me like napalm. I
do not turn away, though I desperately want and need
to. I stay with it. This is my act of love.*

*But it is not the experience of death that Eva Marie
wants from me. It is the acceptance of the experience of
death. This requires another step in the process, another
level of commitment, a further effort of both will and
will-lessness.*

*"Nothing's happening. Should I be feeling something?
Alex?"*

Bella emits a harsh, prolonged gurgle. I haven't
heard that sound from her before, or from any baby,
and the acoustics of the cave make it even more startling. Waves of horror wash over me.

I don't want to stop reading the handbook, for fear
its spell will be broken and I'll lose my chance to get
into it. I'm not likely to be able to figure out what's
wrong with the baby at this particular moment, much
less what to do about it. But I can't ignore her.

Laying the handbook face-up and open on the
ground, I kneel beside Bella. Her eyes are wide open,
bulging. White flecks have formed in the corners
of her mouth. At awkward angles beside her ears,
her fists are opening and closing in what looks like
agitation, and inside the swaddling blanket her feet
and knees flail weakly like kittens in a sack.

I'm afraid to touch her, afraid not to. "What's wrong, little girl?" I coo, pointlessly. "Bella, sweetheart, what's wrong?"

Mostly what I want at this moment is for her to stop—stop making that awful noise, stop contorting, stop needing some impossible thing from me. Or, I realize, to be able to pour directly into her brain and heart some magic healing essence that will make it easier for her to live or easier for her to die—one or the other or both.

When I try to pick her up, she stiffens and I'm afraid I'll drop her. When I hastily lay her back down, she wails as if in anguish. I stroke her back. She flinches away from me. I sit on my haunches without touching her and just watch, not knowing what I'm watching for or to what I'm bearing witness, trying just to be here.

After a while the noise and movement stop as abruptly as they began, and Bella is quiet, eyes still wide open, fists still at her ears but limp now and still. She's not asleep, or dead, but it doesn't seem to me that she's actually conscious, either.

Knees creaking, I ease myself back to the handbook, trying not to disturb her, having no idea what in this world disturbs or pleases her or enters into her awareness at all. After a while, I resume reading.

PROTOCOL
2. SENDER ALLOWS MENTAL SUB-
STANCE TO GATHER INTO PURE AND
HIGHLY PRESSURIZED CONCENTRATE.

"Alex?"

Dimly I am aware of my name being spoken, but there is no need to respond, no response to be made. The ecstasy I have not experienced in many, many years is now suffusing me: apprehension of how it would be to accept mortality, one's own personal mortality, my own, is transcendent joy. I yearn to keep it for myself. But I will not. My purpose in this life is to give the most important things to others, at the greatest possible cost to myself.

I must wait, however, for the exact moment when the excruciating pressure has built to the very verge of explosion, until the essence of the thing is as pure and concentrated as I am able to tolerate and the danger is poised at its most intense level. I am old and frail and out of practice, but somehow I must wait, despite the shaking and nausea, despite the pain and panic and terrible yearning. I must wait.

Bella is moaning. The small eerie sound doesn't come close to filling the cave. Holding her may not be the right thing, but it's all I know to do. It occurs to me that I can probably hold her and read the handbook at the same time. Very gently, although I don't know how I could possibly hurt her now, I lay her across my lap and the handbook open on her torso. When the cover flops over her face I hastily adjust it, but there's no alteration in the sound she's making, and I bend close, put my ear and then my lips to her distorted rosebud mouth, to assure myself that it's really coming from her. Even then, I'm not entirely sure.

For a while, though, I don't read. I just wait. I'm just still. The baby's moans are hollow, like tiny drumbeats. I can't escape them. I can't get enough of them. They pulse and ache, pulse and ache, pulse.

PROTOCOL
3. SENDER GATHERS MENTAL SUB-
STANCE INTO THIN, FLEXIBLE, CYLIN-
DRICAL FORM SUITABLE FOR TRANS-
FER AND INFUSION.

Moaning emanates from one or both of us, Eva Marie and myself, giving voice to the pressure that will surely tear us both apart if it goes on one second too long, but that will cause this entire enterprise to fail if released one second too soon. So focused am I on the gathering that I am hardly aware of being focused, hardly aware at all, until the mental substance begins as if of its own will to take the wire-like form that will allow its transfer from me to the other, from me to Eva Marie. There is the sensation of deep internal burning. I stay with it.

PROTOCOL

4. SENDER TRANSFERS MENTAL
SUBSTANCE INTO RECIPIENT. IF RE-
SISTANCE IS ENCOUNTERED, HEAT
AND FORCE ARE INCREMENTALLY
INCREASED. CARE MUST BE TAKEN TO
FILL RECEIVING VESSEL TO CAPACITY
BUT NOT BEYOND.

No shit. This is why I left him and stayed away for so long. I was afraid he would fill me with his plans for my life, his determination of what and who I should be, beyond my capacity to contain it, until I, the "vessel," would just blow apart.

And he knew it. Here is evidence that all along he knew the danger he was putting me in.

Something is swelling in me. I recognize it. As a child, I often had this ballooning, pressurized sensation, the feeling of being expanded and carried to a chosen place. Later, I would frame it as doing what life expected of me, often for no reason other than that I could. Finding relatives in the Old Country because I knew they were there to be found, though it took years. Keeping in touch with old friends because not to do so would have been stupid and morally wrong. Profoundly loving Martin because I was able to.

Sometimes it has been nothing short of a calling. Adopting my kids was like that; mothering them is, too, never mind that frequently it's also a pain in the ass. Writing used to be like that; it would drive me to the computer in the middle of the night possessed by a story to be told, a character to be developed, a word not to be lost.

Something is growing in me now. It's happening again. Bella is fighting for breath. Her eyes roll back in her head, then roll forward and dart from side to side, focusing on no one thing, taking in everything or nothing through her baby-fine skin.

Is she dying? Am I to help her die? Or is she fighting for life and I am being called to assist?

Daddy, you fucking old wizard, tell me what I'm supposed to do.

Eva Marie gasps, "I can't!" but we are not yet quite at that point. Full, rich, solid acceptance of death is streaming out of me into her, and there is more of it, more space in her for it to fill, more space in me to be emptied.

Indeed, something may be wrong, something for which I am not prepared may be taking place, for Eva Marie's receptive capacity is considerably greater than I would have predicted. The mental substance flows and flows, and she is moaning as if in erotic ecstasy, and now I cannot stop it, now one of us may well implode or explode, now it is beyond me and I fear it is going too far.

Eva Marie and I are in each other's arms.

PROTOCOL

5. AT THE PRECISE MOMENT OF FULL
BUT NOT OVER-CAPACITY, SENDER
STOPS THE FLOW OF MENTAL SUB-
STANCE. TRANSFER COMPLETE. RE-
CIPIENT NOW POSSESSES ALL OF THE
MENTAL SUBSTANCE IN QUESTION,
SENDER NONE.

Whatever it is that I thought was flowing into me must in fact be flowing through me, because I can feel its entrance and exit wounds. It's a stream, a semi-liquid snake hissing and swiftly slithering. It hurts.

Bending over the handbook and the baby, I feel a change in Bella.

The flow stops when it is done. I am emptied, Eva Marie trembles and struggles for air, but neither of us is destroyed. I have done what I can do, and it is good.

Eva Marie whispers, "Thank you, Alex."

I can't do this.

I won't do this. Fuck you, Daddy. "No!" I shout to him. "No!"

"Yes!"

"Alex?"

"Goddamn it, yes!"

I am not, after all, emptied. Eva Marie has taken all she can hold, but Alexandra—somewhere, Alexandra—must be given more. As always, always, she asks too much of me.

The substance that has been flowing through me has stopped. Gratified that I have enough self-determination to say no to my father, at the same time I panic at the prospect of refusing the call.

Bella's gurgling becomes a prolonged shriek and her back arches wildly, snapping her head. I put her down and she writhes and screams. I put my hands on either side of her rigid little body and she flails, bellows, contorts.

I pull myself away from Eva Marie, who does not want to let me go, and curl into a foetal position on the floor. "Do it! Alexandra, you can do this! Now, now, you must do it!"

Abruptly the baby goes still.

Forcing my face as close to hers as possible without actually touching, I can see she is alive. Her blue eyes flicker, and for an instant they seem to focus on mine. From her grotesque rosebud of a mouth comes breath. The longing to feel her heartbeat in my fingers is almost overpowering.

I struggle to my hands and knees and crawl until I am at the entrance to my father's cursed laboratory, on the very verge of escape into and, with any luck, through the yellow wood, when something pierces me. I crouch there. Bella lies still and awake on the dirt floor. Awkwardly I move to her. I kneel over her and she is lightly swaddled in my shadow.

A hot, viscous substance floods into me—from my father; I know it's from my father—and through me and into her. What am I giving her? What am I allowing him to give to her? It doesn't matter. There's nothing I can do to stop it now.

Together, a two-part ragged harmony, Bella and I begin to keen.

"Yes!"

"Sandi?"

Chapter 15

The Koves have gathered to see me off. I'm going home today.

There's a slant to the light and crispness to the air, abruptly, from one day to the next. It's the first morning of autumn, no matter what the calendar says. Just the words "autumn" and "morning" set off both homesickness sharp as cider and the rich deep comfort of knowing I'll soon be home.

That place, home, isn't yellow. In a few weeks it will be, yellow and red and orange, the oak leaves lobed burgundy. But there that's a brief season, not a state of being.

Bella's and my suitcases, laptop, briefcase, diaper bag are in the back of Will's pick-up. Bella herself is in the Snugli on my chest, where I can see and smell and touch her. I'm sitting on Emily's deck surrounded by family. I miss them already, and I can hardly wait to get out of here. We're having a barbecue, of course.

Daddy, though, isn't here. Mom isn't here, either; she's gone back to her husband, which is as it should be. Whether I'll keep in touch with her from now on remains to be seen. Daddy's absence means something, though as usual I don't know what. Vaughn told me he refused to come. He hasn't spoken to me since he found out I was leaving and taking the baby with me. I don't know what his problem is. I thought that's what I was supposed to do. Regardless, it's what I'm doing.

"Will you take her?" Emily asked me that afternoon when we'd made our way back from our father's cave to his house. We'd gotten ourselves and Bella to the couch, the same red couch where Emily and I used to sit and play checkers or dolls or cars, to watch *Star Trek* and *Gunsmoke* and clandestine cartoons Daddy had banned because they would damage our minds, later to make out with our boyfriends on the rare occasions when we had them and at the same time.

Emily had made no move to take her daughter when I'd offered her, so I was holding her. Bella had stopped flailing and making alarming sounds. Her eyes had stopped that awful darting and rolling, too, and I was thinking they might even have lit on me. Certainly she was not responding at all to her mother, who was not responding at all to her.

"Take her?" I echoed. "You mean raise her?"

My sister gave a bitter laugh. "Oh, come on, Sandi, you know she won't live long enough to raise."

I couldn't believe I wasn't just flat-out refusing. "Em, she's your child," I tried. But I heard in my own voice how much I wanted this baby, now that she'd mentioned it, and I was sure she heard it, too.

Again, I held Bella out to her. A look of horror came over her face, and she actually recoiled, which triggered in me a fierce protective instinct. As I gathered the baby back into a snug embrace, her mother said, "I'm pregnant."

I stared at her. "How did that happen?"

"How do you think?"

"But you've been hiding in your room, staying away from everybody. Earl was worried—"

"I went to him. Three times, just to be sure."

"You did this on purpose."

"Sure. Having babies is what I do." A shadow passed over her already shadowed face. "As long as I can. I don't know what happens after that."

"You already have a baby to take care of."

"I can't take care of an infant like this—" she gestured toward the baby without looking at her—"and another at the same time. And I can't do it while I'm pregnant, either. Being pregnant isn't as easy as it used to be."

"What does Earl say?"

"He doesn't want her, either," she declared, sending chills down my back.

"That's a terrible thing to say."

"A terrible thing to feel, too."

"What about the other kids?"

"Alexandra." She put her hand on my wrist in a gesture more threatening than affectionate, avoiding at all costs any contact with her daughter in the process. "If you don't take her, we're going to put her somewhere. Earl's already looking into it."

My mind was reeling from the harshness of Emily's words and the enormity of what she was proposing. I knew there were countless questions I should be asking. "What about custody and—"

"We'll sign over legal custody or give you guardianship or relinquish our rights so you can adopt her if that's what you want. We'll pay you child support—not much, I have to tell you, with eight other kids to support, not anywhere near what our insurance would pay an institution. But we'll do what we can as long as we have to."

"You just want to be rid of her."

Emily's face and body were rigid, her voice cold and strong. "This isn't what I do. This is what you do."

"I can't just—"

She withdrew her hand and got to her feet. "So talk to Martin. Talk to your kids. Talk to your damn therapist. I don't care, whatever you need to do to make your decision. We've made ours."

I brought up the idea to Martin by email, trying to make my case without pushing him into anything.

He wasn't as surprised as I'd thought he be, or as opposed as I'd both feared and hoped. Online and on the phone, we discussed practicalities and legalities like custody, insurance coverage, work schedules and child care options, sleeping arrangements and other household modifications. We went back and forth about how the dog would be with a baby, how Tara and Ramon would be, whether we were too old to be starting with another child, especially given that we'd never had a baby and never especially wanted one, how we would educate ourselves to parent a severely disabled child. We tried to help each other imagine how this would change our lives.

In a family meeting via conference phone call, Tara said, "Will she be my baby sister?"

I said, "Sort of," at the same time Martin said, "Yes."

"Cool."

Ramon said, "Whatever," and I could imagine his shrug. When he got off the phone Martin promised to try to talk to him some more, but neither of us was optimistic about that.

I consulted with her doctor, got records and referrals. Martin gathered information online. We located paediatric specialists, PT and OT services, and parent support groups in our area. We prepared. But all of this had to do with how we would be Bella's parents, not whether. There was never really any question that we'd take her. Of course we would.

When I told Emily, she just nodded. When I told our father, he turned stony. I couldn't tell our mother because she'd already gone home.

So now I sit in the crisp slanted sunshine on Emily's deck, holding my child, while the family gathering for which I am the excuse—more accurately, my imminent departure—goes on around me. Without me, really. Without Daddy, too. Where is he? I think of the cave and maybe should go in search of him there. But Bella is asleep in my arms. Bella, in my arms.

Once past the boundary from yellow wood into cave, the time of day and season are of little note. Herpie's three-curved S flickers at my feet. Notebooks, reference books, blue- and red-lidded plastic boxes labelled in code, jars and sandwich bags with concoctions and raw ingredients for concoctions, stones of various shapes—the place is familiar. Is a familiar. I sit here as I have sat countless times before.

The difference is that now I am done. Nothing else can be asked of me.

Extending my right arm, I grasp at random the first container with which my hand comes in contact, open and overturn it. From the odour and consistency I recognize an elixir I once thought might have a meritorious effect on Galen's social activism, when in his mid-thirties I observed it to be flagging; I have saved it like so much else, for possible future use, but I have no use for it now. It makes a small, short-lived puddle.

Reaching out again, I encounter a stack of books, take one off the top, and with no urge to read even the title, remove pages as many at a time as my arthritic fingers will handle. It is a short book, paperback, and its dismemberment does not take long.

By leaning forward only slightly, I can reach one of the baby-wipe bins. With some effort I pry open its lid. The aromatic granular substance inside makes a scum on the surface of the damp spot where the spilled liquid has sunk into the ground.

My eyes have shut. Both my hands reach out into the space contained by the cave, containing me and my life's work. My left hand finds a row of jars. My right hand finds more books. One of each I bring into my lap, where I pour out the contents of the jar and tear out the contents of the book. Then my hands go back for more.

This is in no way an act of violence. The rhythm of it is gentle, dreamy. Sad, perhaps, but with a deep sense of, if not peace, correctness. This is the finishing. I am finished.

Everything I can reach from where I sit I destroy in this way, and then crawl and slide in a wider and deeper arc, closer to the opening into the yellow wood, deeper into the cave. Joints ache. Skin and flesh are abraded. I can feel the strain on internal organs—heart, lungs, intestines, brain. The floor of the cave is pocked and littered and scoured with what have long been the tools and evidence of my life and are now debris. Stretched out among it, Herpie is of no help at all.

Earl yells that the chicken's ready, and people head for him where he stands in barbecue smoke with long fork and spoon upraised. I watch this steady, taciturn man, wondering who he is and knowing I'll never know, trying to imagine what I'll tell Bella about him if she ever needs to know.

I haven't been able to talk to him about Bella. Whenever I approach him, he leaves the vicinity. I don't know what to make of the fact that he can stand there in his silly barbecue apron swigging a beer and brushing sauce on chicken breasts. I keep thinking I have a responsibility to force the issue with him, but I don't know how. I'm not hungry, and I don't like barbecues.

Various of Earl and Emily's other children have come to say good-bye, maybe urged by their mother. They say good-bye to me, not in any noticeable way to their baby sister. Elizabeth gave me a small framed photo she'd taken of all of us when I first got here, before Mom came and left again, before Bella was born. Erin gave me her email address to give to her cousin Tara. Now it's Evan. Sent by his mother for more napkins, he pauses on his way into the house to give me a solemn hug. Though it's from the side and his little arms don't touch the baby, I want to think it could be meant for both of us.

Will takes the deck chair beside me, balancing a paper plate overloaded with food, including three ears of his homegrown sweet corn. "You're not eating?"

"I'm waiting till the crowd thins."

"Hah. You'll starve that way. Let me get you something."

"No, Will, sit and talk to me."

"Well, here, at least take one of these." He hands me a bright yellow ear of corn.

Holding the corn by the end in one hand, the other being occupied with stroking Bella, I bite into it. Even without butter and salt it's delicious, and with my mouth full I tell him so.

"It's kind of disappointing, actually. From my research on the web, I expected it to be a lot sweeter."

"Oh, Will, give it a rest."

"Can I hold her?"

He's her uncle. This is a perfectly natural and reasonable request, a sweet impulse. But I'm leery.

At my hesitation, Will picks up his plate from where he'd set it on the deck and takes a messy bite of chicken. "Sorry. You're right. I know she's pretty fragile."

"Actually," I say, taking yet another in what will no doubt be an infinite series of risks with this child, "she's not all that fragile. You've had babies. You know what to do. Just support her head."

As fluidly as possible, I ease her out of the Snugli, kiss her in blessing or encouragement or Godspeed, and pass her over to Will. He holds her lightly, one big hand cupping her head as if it were a harvest from his garden, good but not good enough. Bella hasn't reacted to the move.

"Wow," Will says softly, and I reply, "I know."

Amid the general hubbub, we sit for a time in a pocket of companionable silence.

Then strangely rapid thumping punches out of the nearby yellow woods. A bass drum, I realize, and then I realize: Vaughn. Bella stirs fitfully. My head throbs. Will says, "Shit," and gets to his feet. "Here, you better take her."

"What *is* that?" I slide the trembling baby into the Snugli on my chest, where my belly supports her and I can feel the skitter of her heart.

Galen has already left by the gate in the high back fence; it bothers me that he didn't shut it behind him. From her place beside her husband at the barbecue grill, Emily is visibly trying to decide what to do. As he steps down off the deck, Will tells me around a last hasty mouthful of sweet corn he's grabbed for the road what I should already have known: "Something's wrong with Dad."

I've had it with chasing through the damn woods

after Daddy. I have better things to do now. I've always had better things to do. "Fuck it," I snarl, not quite under my breath, and am mortified when Evan, on his delayed return trip from the house with napkins, points at me, and giggles and runs to tell his mom on me.

Emily bends to listen to him, says something and tousles his hair. He runs off. Emily says something to Earl then makes her way out of the yard. She doesn't shut the gate, either. The drumbeat goes on, rhythm and volume disturbingly irregular.

I give up. Tossing the corn into the yard for the dogs, I hold Bella close as I scramble to my feet and hurry to join my sister and brothers.

I feel them coming. Eyes closed, I see them at the place where the paths diverge, or converge, depending on one's perspective. As the first of them reach the edge of the clearing, the arrhythmic drumbeat fills my ears, silly and stirring and sinister. Branches snap. The odour of decomposing yellow-leaf mulch rises from under their feet. Voles burrow wildly underneath. There is no sign of Herpie among them, for my children need no guide to find me here. The yellow wood is small, really. It will not be necessary for me to wait long.

I snap off a branch and whack at tree trunks and rocks as we pass them. Nobody objects. "Daddy is a bastard," I try, but the ugly chant doesn't work anymore.

Emily has fallen behind. She calls, "Hey, you guys, wait up," but we don't. Vaughn's drumbeat is irregular, random, just whenever he feels like thumping—not at all like a heartbeat or a march, but it keeps us going.

That, and Daddy.

What is this place?

I do not know where I am. Yet it seems I have been here many times before, making the disorientation doubly acute. Pain flashes in my chest and my extremities tingle.

I do not know what this is I am holding in my hands. I have the sense that I have known what it is, but now I do not. It is an utterly alien object, with no name I can summon, no intent.

It has heft and many separate pieces. It has rows of black marks on white background, a few x's, many d's, the rest in a strange coded script.

I have begun the concentrated arm and shoulder and wrist movement required to fling the object away when its name and nature come to me: This is the book I have been writing all my life. Pulling handfuls of pages out of the box, I intend to hurl them, but they flutter and scatter and settle yellow in the ambient light.

Nauseous and dizzy, I lower myself to a prone position, hoping to forestall an outright collapse. The floor of the cave is hard and dry to the touch but smells damp, smells yellow. The floor of the cave. The cave.

I crawl on hands and knees until I cannot, then crawl on my belly, making little progress. Things fall. Things spill and break and crumple. What I had assumed was Herpie turns out to be only her moulted skin.

But something is in my head. Alexandra. There she is.

There he is.

I'm not first in line, but I see him first and leave the path to push past my brothers, tearing through undergrowth and shielding Bella from scratching branches. Behind me Emily cries my name, cries "Bella!"

Daddy's lying at the entrance of his hideout, the top of his bald head grazed by a shaft of pale sunlight through the leaf canopy. Pieces of something white surround him—papers, I realize; pages. Something arcs between us and something viscous starts to move, seeping rather than flowing this time, warm rather than hot, and moving in both directions.

When I lower myself beside him, awkwardly because of my own bulk and the fragile presence of Bella now between us, there's no space for any of the rest of them, and I'm sorry for that, but only dimly. It's not my fault. He set it up this way. Galen starts to orchestrate things, but his orders fizzle. Will breathes, "Shit." Emily is weeping. Vaughn has gone off somewhere and given up the drum for a high sweet flute.

The old chant still plays in my head. Daddy is a wizard—

Here's Bella, Daddy.

The baby.
Bella.
Love her.
I cannot love her. It is more than I can do. But you can.

My father, thin and weak, and the smaller, stronger baby are in my arms. A serpentine ripple runs along my back. The substance he sends into me is only a trickle now, but I need every last drop.

Love her. You must love her. I give it to you. My last gift.

Yes. I will. I accept.
Thank you, Daddy.

ABOUT THE AUTHOR

Melanie Tem's work has received the Bram Stoker, International Horror Guild, British Fantasy, and World Fantasy Awards, and a nomination for the Shirley Jackson Award. She has published numerous short stories, eleven solo novels, two collaborative novels with Nancy Holder, and two collaborative novels and a short story collection with her husband Steve Rasnic Tem. She is also a published poet, an oral storyteller, and a playwright. Solo stories have recently appeared in *Asimov's Science Fiction Magazine*, *Crimewave*, and *Interzone*, and anthologies such as *Black Wings* and *Dangerous Games*.

The Tems live in Denver, CO, where Melanie is executive director of a non-profit independent-living organization. They have four children and six grandchildren.

EMB
RACE
THE
ODD

THE DEAD HAMLETS
PETER ROMAN

Something is rotten in the court of the faerie queen. A deadly spirit is killing off the faerie, and it has mysterious ties to Shakespeare's play, Hamlet. The only one who can stop it is the immortal Cross, a charming rogue who also happens to be a drunk, a thief, and an angel killer. He is no friend of the faerie since they stole his daughter and made her one of their own. He encounters an eccentric and deadly cast of characters along the way: the real Witches of Macbeth, the undead playwright/demon hunter Christopher Marlowe, an eerie Alice from the Alice in Wonderland books, a deranged and magical scholar— and a very supernatural William Shakespeare. When Cross discovers a startling secret about the origins of Hamlet itself, he finds himself trapped in a ghost story even he may not be able to escape alive.

AVAILABLE NOW
ISBN 978-1-77148-316-2

THE HOUSE OF WAR AND WITNESS
LINDA, LOUISE, AND MIKE CAREY

Prussia, 1740. With the whole of Europe balanced on the brink of war, an Austrian regiment is sent to the farthest frontier of the empire to hold the border against the might of Prussia. Their garrison—the ancient house called Pokoj, inhabited by ghosts only Drozde, the quartermaster's mistress, can see. They tell her stories of Pokoj's past, and a looming menace in its future . . . a grim discovery that both Drozde and the humourless lieutenant Klaes are about to stumble upon. It will mean the end of villagers and soldiers alike, and a catastrophe that only the restless dead can prevent. . . .

AVAILABLE NOW

ISBN 978-1-77148-312-4

PROBABLY MONSTERS
RAY CLULEY

From British Fantasy Award-winning author Ray Cluley comes Probably Monsters—a collection of dark, weird, literary horror stories. Sometimes the monsters are bloodsucking fiends with fleshy wings. Sometimes they're shambling dead things that won't rest, or simply creatures red in tooth and claw. But often they're worse than any of these. They're the things that make us howl in the darkness, hoping no one hears. These are the monsters we make ourselves, and they can find us anywhere. . . .

AVAILABLE NOW
ISBN 978-1-77148-334-6